MOTHWISE

MOTHWISE

KNUT HAMSUN

Translated by W.W. Worster

Edited with an introduction
by Richard Eccles

R·H·B

First published in Great Britain as *Mothwise,* by Gyldendal, London, in 1921 from the Norwegian *Svœrmere.*
This edition published 2015 by Red Hand Books

RED HAND BOOKS
Old Bath Road, London SL3 0NS
1618 Yishan Road, Minhang District, 201103 Shanghai
150th Avenue, Springfield Gardens, 11413 New York
Şerifali Mahallesi, Umraniye 34775 Istanbul
Cross Road A, Andheri, 400093 Mumbai

www.rhbks.com

ISBN: 978-1-910346-04-4 (Paperback)

MOTHWISE

Fishglue. This most neglected of products is one of the key elements of *Mothwise* and you may never have read a piece of literature in which it figures so prominently. If you have read any Hamsun before then some of the other constituents may be more familiar: the setting in the far North of Norway where the sun never sets for two or three months that makes people act in such peculiar ways, the tales of love in all its many forms that bind and break across tiny isolated fishing communities and the characters that amuse and irritate and shine and disappoint that live and breathe from beginning to all-too-soon an end.

Hamsun himself might have felt more affinity with fishglue than might be obvious: his marriage of six years to Bergljot is falling apart, he has no home and nowhere to write, he hardly sees his barely two year old child, it's six years since his last novel came out, his recent play has been refused by major producers and he is having to ask around colleagues to borrow money to survive as well as being seriously in debt. He cannot settle anywhere. He is drawn repeatedly to flirting outrageously with married and unmarried women and drawn into vitriolic exchanges with the leading political and literary figures of his day about the union with Sweden amongst other things. Before and after July 1904 when this book comes out Hamsun is the talk of two towns, Copenhagen and Kristiania (Oslo). He is stuck no matter which way he turns.

Ove Rolandsen, the guitar-playing, big-nosed and big-voiced character at the centre of this little romantic comedy of a novel is the lighter side of Hamsun's psyche. After twenty one years away Hamsun had taken a trip up north just four years earlier to his childhood home in Hamarøy where his mother and father still lived. Hamsun was struck by the poverty and the changes that had taken place: people in debt for things they once hadn't needed, people buying goods in shops that once they had lived without or made themselves. And many of the people whom he had known and loved were now dead or gone. When one review in 1904 complained that this was merely a repetition of characters and situations that Hamsun has already created he was not wrong; but something else was happening, which would lead to greatness.

Strangely then, *Mothwise*, or *Svaermere* in the original, came to life in a little pension in Ås, forty kilometres south of Kristiania. It took him less than two months to write perhaps because it is quite short. On the front cover of my cheap copy (75 NOK) is a rather compelling painting of a very upright woman in a red dress just left of centre sitting opposite a man, pushed to the right-hand edge. The centre of the painting is the fire burning with tongues of red and yellow flames on the beach under a beautiful sunlit night sky. Inside it tells me that it is a new edition, 1999 and published by Gyldendal in their Pocket series. Ninety five years earlier Hamsun had been told by Gyldendal's Literary Director, Peter Nansen, to write something all the family could read without upsetting anyone, fewer than one hundred pages and in the style of good old Jonas Lie, a sort of Norwegian Dickens. For 2,000 kroner. Let's make people like Hamsun again, seems to have been the plan.

Perhaps the jury is still out more than a century later. But this is Hamsun in transition as an artist. He's no longer the sufferer at the centre of the psychological wrestling match as in *Hunger* or *Pan*, he's stepped back, he's watching from a distance as his characters swarm and dream around one another. And it's funny. When the price of *sild* goes up lowly Olga can put on airs and graces. There's the running joke of the Priest's wife's shabby shoes. Hamsun is moving indeed into Dicken's territory: irony, mockery, running jokes, a realism that reveals why people do what they do in the social terrain they have to move in and plots that move swiftly on but are grounded in a reality that would be recognised. Hamsun is no social reformer but he has sympathy. He has seen himself and other people trapped by circumstance and poverty and to all his characters disaster is only one wrong move away. So Rolandsen is partly Hamsun, challenging all conventions and all the niceties of received behaviour in the most deliberately outlandish but well-meant ways. And feeling often so misunderstood, like Hamsun himself.

And the women, the beautiful women… Time after time Hamsun has written about love and all its ecstasies and depths and how it always leads to unhappiness. How love and happiness are incompatible. People who fate and perhaps self will not allow to be together. The beautiful women who he has so eloquently created who are out of reach and ultimately unknowable and exalted and then cast down within the same paragraph. But this time it will be different, just. On the road to fulfilment Rolandsen is shadowed by his nemesis, the Priest, the unnamed representative of moral authority that Hamsun has fought with all of his life, the moralising do-gooder who even in reality is all around him taking many forms: the priests, the Headmasters, the politicians, the husbands, the lawyers, the creditors, the critics. Not to mention the poison-pen letter writers and half-mad stalkers who had ruined his life as recently as 1897. *Mothwise* is all light with an undertone of dark rebellion in its main protagonist. He throws down challenges to God and orthodoxy, 'He's Lord of all creation, I know, but I shouldn't think there's anything much in being just a God of beasts and mountains. After all, it's us human beings that make Him what He is.' says Rolandsen to the Priest's wife. He drinks openly, he sings songs in the middle of the night to other men's wives and he likes a bit of a fight. And he finds success with that most unlikely substance we started with.

Despite its weaknesses and its lightness *Mothwise* is beautifully constructed and orchestrated. The range of characters who react in such pre-ordained and natural ways shadow one another in ironic patterns. And the lack of detail as important as the memorable detail: the squeaky church shoes, the buttons and sashes and brooches, the nameless lady with the doe-eyes, the featureless Jomfru van Loos, the importance of appearance and the shifts in language as each character fights for space as Hamsun takes us there and makes us care. Hamsun knows what he is writing about even as he does it a thousand miles away. He knows about rank and convention and hard work and the value of food and the value of reputation. How often the novel concerns itself with 'what sort of man he was.' This world is alive with rumours, gossips, grumblings, worries and fly comments, social life in all its shifting forms. Hamsun is moving towards a different world view and a new way of writing about it.

The title itself is problematic. Filmed as *Telegrafisten*, The Telegraphist, translated by Worster in this present edition as *Mothwise* and elsewhere as *Dreamers* the title deserves some attention. *Svaermere* can mean dreamers, swarmers and also butterflies and moths. Hamsun had what to us might seem a curiously unnationalistic view that the written language of Norway should be Danish. Just before *Mothwise* was written the Swedes, who ruled Norway at the time, had threatened Norway with war in order to preserve the Union. It was only in 1905 that Norway achieved independence, which it had effectively lost six hundred years earlier. In that intervening period it had become impossible to describe in any clear way what defined standard Norwegian. Even today there are two main languages that are Norwegian and within each of the broad divisions are multitudinous dialects. And Hamsun exploits this. Worster has his work cut out conveying the nuances of Hamsun's language. This language is full of archaisms, dialectal words, Danish words, terms that belong to distinct classes or trades and poetic variations of many types. He should also be forgiven for sounding old-fashioned himself and at times ever so slightly prudish. The translations were being published in America at a time when no one else would touch them. I have tried to point out some examples of the sorts of effects that Worster's language choices reflect concerning the translator's art. Often he surpasses even Hamsun himself: *som den flotte handelskonge han var*, literally, like the great business-king he was, becomes in Worster's hands, like the open-handed merchant-prince he was. And how oddly beautiful are Worster's final sentences of Chapter 2: But now it was spring again. And the spring was a thing well-nigh intolerable to a great heart. It drove creation to its uttermost limit; ay, it blew with spiced winds into innocent nostrils.

RICHARD ECCLES

I

Marie van Loos, housekeeper at the Vicarage, stands by the kitchen window looking out far up the road. She knows the couple there by the fence—knows them indeed, seeing 'tis no other than Telegraph-Rolandsen, her own betrothed, and Olga the parish clerk's daughter. It is the second time she has seen those two together this spring— now what does it mean? Save that Jomfru van Loos had a host of things to do just now, she would have gone straight up to them that moment and demanded an explanation.

As it was, how could she? There was no time for anything now, with the whole place upside down, and the new priest and his lady expected any minute. Young Ferdinand is already posted at an upstairs window to keep a look-out to seaward, and give warning as soon as the boat is in sight, so that the coffee can be ready the moment the travellers arrive. And they would need it, after coming all the way from Rosengaard, four miles off. Rosengaard is the nearest place at which the steamer calls, and from there they come on by boat.

There is still a trifle of snow and ice about, but it is May now, and the weather fine, with long, bright days over Nordland. The crows are getting on fast with their nests, and the new green grass is sprouting on the bare hummocks. In the garden, the sallows were in bud already, for all they were standing in snow.

The great question now was what the new priest would be like. All the village was burning to know. True, he was only coming as chaplain for the time being, till a permanent incumbent was appointed; but such temporary chaplains might often remain for a considerable time in a place like this, with its poor fisher population, and a heavy journey to the annex church every fourth Sunday. It was by no means the sort of living anyone would grasp at for a permanency.

It was rumoured that the newcomers to the Vicarage were wealthy folk, who did not need to think twice about every *skilling* they spent. They had already engaged a housekeeper and two maids in advance; and they had not been sparing of help for the field work either, but taken on two farm-hands, besides young Ferdinand, who was to be smart and obliging, and make himself generally useful. All felt it was a blessing to the congregation to have a pastor so comfortably off. Such a man, of course, would not be over-strict in the matter of tithes and other dues; far from it; he would doubtless reach out a helping hand to those in need. Altogether, there was a great deal of excitement. The lay-helpers and other fishermen had turned out in readiness, and were down at the boat-sheds now, tramping up and down in their heavy boots, chewing tobacco, spitting, and exchanging observations.

Here comes Big Rolandsen at last, striding down the road. He had left Olga behind, and Jomfru van Loos withdrew from her kitchen window once more. Oh, but she would have a word with him about it, never fear; it was no uncommon thing for her to have matters outstanding with Ove Rolandsen. Jomfru van Loos was of Dutch extraction, she spoke with a Bergen accent, and was so hasty of speech at times that Rolandsen himself had been driven to give her the nickname of Jomfru *Fan los.** Big Rolandsen was always witty, and very often improper.

And where was he off to now? Was it his quite remarkable intention to go down and meet the Vicarage people himself? Likely as not he was no more sober now than many a time before. There he was, walking down, with a twig of budding

---

* The devil run loose.

sallow in his buttonhole, and his hat a thought on one side—going to meet them like that! The lay-helpers down at the waterside were by no means glad of his company at the moment—at this particular, highly important moment.

Was it right or proper, now, for a man to look like that? His red nose had an air of pride ill-suited to his humble station; and, more than that, it was his habit to let his hair grow all through the winter, till his head grew more and more artistic. Jomfru van Loos, who owed him a sharp word or so, declared that he looked like a painter who had come down in the world, and ended as a photographer. Four-and-thirty was Rolandsen now, a student, and a bachelor; he played the guitar, trolled out the local songs with a deep voice, and laughed till the tears flowed at all the touching parts. That was his lordly way. He was in charge of the telegraph station, and had been here now for ten years in the same place. A tall fellow, powerfully built, and ready enough to lend a hand in a brawl.

Suddenly young Ferdinand gives a start. From his attic window he catches sight of Trader Mack's white houseboat hurrying round the point; next moment he is down the stairs in three break-neck strides, shouting through to the kitchen, "Here they come!"

Then he hurries out to tell the farm-hands. The men drop the things they are holding, slip on their Sunday jackets with all speed, and hasten down to the waterside to help, if needed. That made ten in all to welcome the new arrivals.

"*Goddag!*" says the chaplain from the stern, smiling a little, and doffing his soft hat. All those on shore bare their heads respectfully, and the lay-helpers bow till their long hair falls over their eyes. Big Rolandsen is less obsequious than the others; he stands upright as ever, but takes off his hat and holds it low down.

The chaplain is a youngish man, with reddish whiskers and a spring crop of freckles; his nostrils seem to be choked with a growth of fair hair. His lady is lying down in the deck-house, sea-sick and miserable.

"We're there now," says her husband in through the doorway, and helps her out. Both of them are curiously dressed, in thick, old clothes that look far from elegant. Still, these, no doubt, are just some odd over-things they have borrowed for the journey; their own rich clothes will be inside, of course. The lady has her hat thrust back, and a pale face with large eyes looks out at the men. Lay-helper Levion wades out and carries her ashore; the priest manages by himself.

"I'm Rolandsen, of the Telegraph," says Big Rolandsen, stepping forward. He was not a little drunk, and his eyes glared stiffly, but being a man of the world, there was no hesitation in his manner. Ho, that Rolandsen, a deuce of a fellow! No one had ever seen him at a loss when it came to mixing with grand folk, and throwing out elegant bits of speech. "Now if only I knew enough," he went on, addressing the priest, "I might introduce us all. Those two there, I fancy, are the lay-helpers. These two are your farm-hands. And this is Ferdinand."

And the priest and his wife nod round to all. *Goddag! Goddag!* They would soon learn to know one another. Well ... the next thing would be to get their things on shore.

But Lay-helper Levion looks hard at the deck-house, and stands ready to wade out once more. "Aren't there any little ones?" he asks.

No answer; all turn towards the priest and his wife.

"If there won't be any children?" asks the lay-helper again.

"No," says the boatman.

The lady flushed a little. The chaplain said:

"There are only ourselves.... You men had better come up

and I'll settle with you now."

Oh, a rich man, of course. A man who would not withhold his due from the poor. The former priest never "settled" with people at all; he only said thanks, and that would be all "for now."

They walked up from the quay, Rolandsen leading the way. He walked by the side of the road, in the snow, to leave place for the others; he wore light shoes, in his vain and showy way, but it did not seem to hurt him; he even walked with his coat unbuttoned, for all it was only May and the wind cold.

"Ah, there's the church," says the priest.

"It looks old," says his wife. "I suppose there's no stove inside?" she asks.

"Why, I can't say for certain," answers Rolandsen. "But I don't think so."

The priest started. This man, then, was no church-goer, but one who made little distinction between week-day and Sabbath. And he grew more reserved thenceforward.

Jomfru van Loos is standing on the steps; Rolandsen introduces her as well. And, having done so, he takes off his hat and turns to go.

"Ove! Wait a minute!" whispered Jomfru van Loos.

But Rolandsen did not wait a minute; he took off his hat once more and retired backwards down the steps. Rather a curious person, thought the priest.

Fruen† had gone inside at once. She was feeling a little better now, and began taking stock of the place. The nicest and lightest room she assigned to her husband as a study, and reserved to herself the bedroom Jomfru van Loos had occupied before.

---

† The mistress—i.e., the priest's wife. A married lady is often referred to as *Fruen*, or addressed as *Frue*. In the present book, the name of the priest is not stated; he is referred to throughout as *Præsten*, and his wife as *Præstefruen*, or *Fruen* simply.

II

No, Rolandsen did not wait a minute; he knew his Jomfru van Loos, and had no doubt as to what she wanted. Rolandsen was not easily persuaded to anything he did not care about himself.

A little way along the road he met a fisherman who had come out too late to be present at the arrival. This was Enok, a pious, inoffensive man, who always walked with downcast eyes and wore a kerchief tied round his head for earache.

"You're too late," said Rolandsen as he passed.

"Has he come?"

"He has. I shook hands with him." Rolandsen passed on, and called back over his shoulder, "Enok, mark what I say. *I envy that man his wife!*"

Now saying a foolish and most improper thing like that to Enok was choosing the very man of all men. Enok would be sure to bring it about.

Rolandsen walked farther and farther along by the wood, and came to the river. Here was the fish-glue factory, owned by Trader Mack; some girls were employed on the place, and it was Rolandsen's way to chaff them as often as he passed. He was a very firebrand for that, and none could deny it. Moreover, he was in high spirits to-day, and stayed longer than usual. The girls saw at once that he was splendidly in drink.

"You, Ragna, what d'you think it is makes me come up here every day?" says Rolandsen.

"I don't know, I'm sure," says Ragna.

"Oh, you think, of course, it's old Mick."

The girls laughed at that. "Old Mick, ha, ha! Old Nick, he means."

"It's for your salvation," says Rolandsen. "You'd better take care of yourself with the fisher-lads about here; they're a wicked lot."

"Wicked, indeed! And what about yourself, then?" says another girl. "With two children of your own already. You ought to be ashamed of yourself."

"Ah, Nicoline, now how can you say such a thing? You've been a thorn in my heart and near the death of me for more than I can say, and that you know. But as for you, Ragna, I'm going to see you saved, and that without mercy."

"You go and talk to Jomfru van Loos," says Ragna.

"But you've desperate little sense," Rolandsen went on. "Now those fish-heads, for instance. How long do you steam them before you screw down the valve?"

"Two hours," says Ragna.

Rolandsen nods to himself. He had reckoned that up and worked it out before. Ho, that firebrand Rolandsen, he knew well enough what it was took him up to the factory every day, chaffing the girls and sniffing about all the time.

"Don't take that lid off, Pernille," he cried suddenly. "Are you out of your senses, girl?"

Pernille flushes red. "Frederik he said I was to stir it round," she says.

"Every time you lift the lid, some of the heat goes out," says Rolandsen.

But a moment later, when Frederik Mack, the trader's son, came up, Rolandsen turned off into his usual jesting tone once more.

"Wasn't it you, Pernille, that was in service at the *Lensmand's* one year, and bullied the life out of everyone in the place?

Smashing everything to bits in a rage—all barring the bedclothes, perhaps."

The other girls laughed; Pernille was the gentlest creature that ever lived, and weakly to boot. Moreover, her father was organ-blower at the church, which gave her a sort of godliness, as it were.

Coming down on to the road again, Rolandsen caught sight of Olga once more—coming from the store, no doubt. She quickened her pace, hurrying to avoid him; it would never do for Rolandsen to think she had been waiting about for him. But Rolandsen had no such idea; he knew that if he did not catch this young maid face to face she would always hurry away and disappear. And it did not trouble him in the least that he made no progress with her; far from it. It was not Olga by any means that filled his mind.

He comes home to the telegraph station, and walks in with his lordliest air, to ward off his assistant, who wanted to gossip. Rolandsen was not an easy man to work with just at present. He shut himself up in a little room apart, that no one ever entered save himself and one old woman. Here he lived and slept.

This room is Rolandsen's world. Rolandsen is not all foolishness and drink, but a great thinker and inventor. There is a smell of acids and chemicals and medicine in that room of his; the smell oozed out into the passage and forced every stranger to notice it. Rolandsen made no secret of the fact that he kept all these medicaments about solely to mask the smell of the quantities of *brændevin* he was always drinking. But that again was Ove Rolandsen's unfathomable artfulness....

The truth of the matter was that he used those liquids in bottles and jars for his experiments. He had discovered a chemical process for the manufacture of fish-glue—a new method that would leave Trader Mack and his factory simply nowhere. Mack had set up his plant at considerable expense; his means of transport were inadequate, and his supplies of raw material restricted to the fishing season. Moreover, the business was superintended by his son Frederik, who was by no means an expert. Rolandsen could manufacture fish-glue from a host of other materials than fish heads, and also from the waste products of Mack's own factory. Furthermore, from the last residue of all he could extract a remarkable dye.

Save for his weight of poverty and helplessness, Rolandsen of the Telegraphs would have made his invention famous by this time. But no one in the place could come by ready money except through the agency of Trader Mack, and, for excellent reasons, it was impossible to go to him in this case. He had once ventured to suggest that the fish-glue from the factory was over-costly to produce, but Mack had merely waved his hand in his lordly, careless way, and said that the factory was a gold-mine, nothing less. Rolandsen himself was burning to show forth the results of his work. He had sent samples of his product to chemists at home and abroad, and satisfied himself that it was good enough so far. But he got no farther. He had yet to give the pure, finished liquid to the world, and take out patents in all countries.

So that it was not without motive and vainly that Rolandsen had turned out that day to receive the new chaplain and his family. Rolandsen, the wily one, had a little plan of his own. For if the priest were a wealthy man, he could, no doubt, invest a little in a safe and important invention. "If no one else will do it, I will"—that was the thing he would say, no doubt. Rolandsen had hopes.

Alas, Rolandsen was always having hopes—a very little was enough to fire him. On the other hand he took his disappointments bravely; none could say otherwise than that he bore himself stiffly and proudly, and was not to be crushed. There was Mack's daughter Elise, for instance, even she had not crushed him. A tall, handsome girl, with a brown skin and red lips, and twenty-three years of age. It was whispered that Captain Henriksen, of the coasting steamer, worshipped her in secret; but years came and years passed, and nothing happened. What could be the matter? Rolandsen had already made an eternal fool of himself three years back; when she was only twenty he had laid his heart at her feet. And she had been kind enough not to understand him. That was where Rolandsen ought to have stopped and drawn back, but he went forward instead, and now, last year, he had begun to speak openly. Elise Mack had been forced to laugh in his face, to make this presumptuous telegraph person realise the gulf between them. Was she not a lady, who had kept no less than Captain Henriksen waiting years for her consent?

And then it was that Rolandsen went off and got engaged to Jomfru van Loos. Ho, he was not the man to take his death of a refusal from high quarters!

But now it was spring again. And the spring was a thing well-nigh intolerable to a great heart. It drove creation to its uttermost limit; ay, it blew with spiced winds into innocent nostrils.

III

The herring are moving in from the sea. The master seiners lie out in their boats, peering through glasses at the water all day long. Where the birds hover in flocks, swooping down now and then to snap at the water, there are the herring to be found; already they can be taken in deep water with the nets. But now comes the question whether they will move up into shallower water, into the creeks and fjords where they can be cut off from retreat by the seine. It is then that the bustle and movement begins in earnest, with shouting and swarming and crowding up of men and ships. And there is money to be made, a harvest in plenty as the sands of the sea.

The fisherman is a gambler. He lays out his nets or his lines, and waits for the haul; he casts his seine and leaves the rest to fate. Often he meets with only loss and loss again, his gear is carried out to sea, or sunk, or ruined by storms, but he furnishes himself anew and tries again. Sometimes he ventures farther off, to some grounds where he has heard of others finding luck, rowing and toiling for weeks over stubborn seas, only to find he has come too late; the fishing is at an end. But now and again the prize may lie waiting for him on his way, and stop him and fill his boat with money. No one can say whom luck will favour next; all have like grounds, or hope....

Trader Mack had everything in readiness; his seine was in the boat, his master seiner swept the offing with his glass. Mack had a schooner and a couple of coasting-boats in the bay, emptied and cleaned after their voyage to Bergen with dried fish; he would load them up with herring now if the herring came; his store-loft was bursting with empty barrels. He was a buyer himself as well, in the market for herrings to any quantity, and he had provided himself with a stock of ready money, to take all he could before the price went up.

Half-way through May, Mack's seine made its first haul. Nothing to speak of, only some fifty barrels, but the catch was noised abroad, and, a few days later, a stranger crew appeared in the bay. Things looked like business.

Then one night there was a burglary at Mack's office in the factory. It was a bold misdemeanour indeed; the nights now were shining bright from evening to morning, and everything could be seen far off. The thief had broken open two doors and stolen two hundred *Daler*.

It was an altogether unprecedented happening in the village, and a thing beyond understanding. To break in and steal from Mack—from Mack himself—even aged folk declared they had never heard the like in their days. The village folk might do a little pilfering and cheating in accordance with their humble station, but burglary on a grand scale was more than they would ever attempt. And suspicion fell at once on the stranger crew, who were questioned closely.

But the stranger crew were able to prove that they had been out, with every man on board, four miles away, on the night.

This was a terrible blow to Trader Mack. It meant that the thief was someone in the village itself.

Trader Mack cared little for the money; he said openly that the thief must have been a fool not to take more. But that any of his own people should steal from him—the idea cut him to the quick, mighty man as he was, and the protector of them all. Did he not furnish half the entire communal budget with the taxes he paid on his various undertakings?—and had any deserving case ever been turned away from his door without relief?

Mack offered a reward for information leading to discovery. Something had to be done. There were strange boats coming in now almost every day, and a nice idea they would gain of the relations between Trader Mack and his people when it was found that they robbed and stole his money. Like the open-handed merchant prince he was, Mack fixed the reward at four hundred *Daler*. Then all could see he was not afraid of putting up a round sum.

The story came to the ears of the new priest, and, on Trinity Sunday, when the sermon was to be about Nicodemus who came to Jesus in the night, he made use of the opportunity to deliver an attack upon the culprit. "Here they come to us by night," he said, "and break open our doors and steal away our means of life. Nicodemus did no wrong; he was a timorous man, and chose the night for his going, but he went on his soul's errand. But what did men do now? Alas, the world had grown in evil-doing, the night was used for plundering and stealing. Let the guilty be punished; bring him forth!"

The new priest was found to be a fighting cock. This was the third time he had preached, and already he had persuaded many of the sinners in the parish to mend their ways. When he stood up in the pulpit, he was so pale and strange that he looked like a madman. Some of the congregation found the first Sunday quite enough, and did not venture to come again. Even Jomfru van Loos was shaken, and that was no little thing. Rough and hard as a rasp was Jomfru van Loos, and had been all her days till now. The two maids under her noted the change with much content.

There was a considerable gathering in the place now. And there were some who were not displeased at the discomfiture of Trader Mack. Mack was getting too mighty a man altogether, with his two trading stations, his seines, his factory, and his numerous vessels; the fisherfolk from other stations held by their own traders, who were condescending and easy to get on with, and who did not affect white collars or deerskin gloves as did Mack. The burglary was no more than he deserved for his high-and-mightiness. And as for offering rewards of so-and-so many hundred *Daler* for this, that, and the other—Mack would be better advised to keep his ready cash for buying herring, if the herring came. After all, his money was not beyond counting; not like the stars in the sky. Who could say but that the whole thing might have been cleverly contrived by himself, or his son Frederik: a sham burglary, to make it appear that he could afford to lose money like grass, while all the time he was in sore need of cash? So the gossip ran among the boats and on shore.

Mack realised that he must make a good impression. Here were folk from five different parishes who would carry back word of what sort of man he was to traders and relatives in other parts. Again and again it must be seen what manner of man was Trader Mack of Rosengaard.

Next time he had occasion to go up to the factory Mack hired a steamer for the journey. It was four miles from the stopping-place, and it cost a deal of money, but Mack took no heed of that. There was a great to-do about the place when the steamer came bustling in with Mack and his daughter Elise on board. He was lord of the vessel, so to speak, and stood there on board with his red sash round his waist, for all it was a summer's day. As soon as father and daughter had landed, the steamer put about and went off at once; all could see that it had come for their sake only. And in face of this, some even of the stranger folk bowed to the power of Mack.

But Mack did more. He could not forget the disgrace of

that burglary affair. He put up a new placard, promising that the reward of four hundred *Daler* would be paid even to the thief himself if he came forward. Surely this was unequalled as a piece of chivalrous generosity? All must admit after this that it was not the money, a few miserable *Daler*, that troubled him. But the gossip was not stilled even now. There were still whisperings: "If the thief's the man I think, you'll see he'll not own up to it now any more than before. But never a word that I said so!"

Mack the all-powerful was in an intolerable position. His reputation was being undermined. For twenty years past he had been the great man of the place, and all had made way for him respectfully; now there seemed to be less of respect in their greetings. And this despite the fact that he had been decorated with a Royal Order. A great man indeed he had been. He was thespokesman of the village, the fishermen worshipped him, the little traders of the outlying stations imitated his ways. Mack had stomach trouble, brought on, no doubt, by his royal table and splendid living, and he wore a broad red sash round his waist as soon as it began to be at all cold. Soon the little traders of the outlying stations began to wear red sashes too, for all they were but insignificant folk—upstarts whom Mack graciously allowed to live. They too would have it appear that they were great men living in luxury, with stomach troubles due to extravagant over-feeding. Mack went to church in shoes that creaked, and walked up the aisle with supercilious noises; but even his creaky shoes were copied by others after him. There were some, indeed, who set their shoes in water and dried them hard for Sundays, to creak emphatically among the congregation. Mack had been the great example in every way.

IV

Rolandsen sits in his laboratory, hard at work. Looking out from the window he marks how a certain branch of a certain tree in the wood moves up and down. Somebody must be shaking it, but the leaves are too thick for him to see more. Rolandsen goes back to his work.

But somehow the work seemed to clog to-day. He took his guitar and tried singing one of his joyful laments, but even that failed to please him. The spring was come, and Rolandsen was troubled.

Elise Mack was come; he had met her the evening before. Proud and haughty she was, and carried herself like a lady; it seemed as if she would have tried to please him a little with a touch of kindliness here and there, but he would have none of it.

"I saw the telegraph people at Rosengaard before I left," she said.

But Rolandsen had no wish to claim friendship with the telegraph people; he was no colleague of theirs. She was trying to emphasise the distance between herself and him once more—ho-ho! He would pay her out for that!

"You must teach me the guitar some day," she said.

Now this was a thing to start at and to accept with thanks. But Rolandsen would have none of it. On the contrary, he would pay her out on the spot. He said:

"Very pleased, I'm sure. Whenever you like. You can have my guitar."

Yes, that was the way he treated her. As if she were any but

Elise Mack, a lady worth ten thousand guitars.

"No, thank you," she said. "But we might use it to practise on."

"I'll make you a present of it."

But at that she tossed her head, and said:

"Thank you; I'd rather be excused."

The wily Rolandsen had touched her there. And then all at once he forgot every thought of paying her out, and murmured:

"I only meant to give you the only thing I had."

And with that he raised his hat and bowed deeply, and walked away.

He walked away to the parish clerk's in search of Olga. The spring was come, and Rolandsen must have a lady-love; 'twas no light thing to rule such a big heart. But apart from that he was paying attention to Olga with a purpose. There was some talk about Frederik Mack, how he had an eye to Olga himself. And Rolandsen meant to cut him out, no less. Frederik was brother to Elise herself, and it would do the family good if one of them were jilted. But anyhow, Olga was attractive enough in herself. Rolandsen had seen her grow up from a slip of a child; there was little money to spare in the home, and she had to wear her clothes as far as they would go before getting new things; but she was a bright, pretty girl, and her shyness was charming.

Rolandsen had met her two days in succession. The only way to manage it was by going straight up to the house and lending her father a book every day. He had to force these books on the old man, who had never asked for them and could not understand them. Rolandsen had to speak up for his books and plead their cause. They were the most useful books in the world, he said, and he, Rolandsen, was bent on making them known, on spreading them abroad. *Værsaagod!**

---

* Literally, "Be so good" (as to accept ...), used when offering anything.

He asked the old man if he could cut hair. But the parish clerk had never cut hair in his life; Olga did all the hair-cutting in the house. Whereupon Rolandsen addressed himself to Olga, with prayers and eloquent entreaties, to cut his hair. Olga blushed and hid herself. "I couldn't," she said. But Rolandsen routed her out again, and overwhelmed her with irresistible words until she agreed.

"How do you like it done?" she asked.

"Just as you like," he answered. "As if I could think of having it otherwise."

Then, turning to her father, he tangled him up in a maze of intricate questions, until the old man could stand no more, and at last withdrew to the kitchen.

Rolandsen, elated, grew more extravagant than ever. He turned to Olga and said:

"When you go out in the dark on a winter evening and come into a lighted room, then all the light comes hurrying from everywhere to gather in your eyes."

Olga did not understand a word of all this, but said, "Yes."

"Yes," said Rolandsen, "and it's the same with me when I come in and see you."

"Is it short enough here now?" asked Olga.

"No, not nearly. Just keep on. Do it just the way you like. Ah, you thought you could slip away and hide—didn't you?—but you couldn't. It was like the lightning putting out a spark."

Of all the mad talk....

"I could manage better if you'd keep your head still," said she.

"Then I can't look at you. Say, Olga, have you a sweetheart?"

Olga was all unprepared for this. She was not so old and experienced as yet but that some things could put her out of countenance.

"Me? No," was all she said. "Now I think it'll have to do as it is. I'll just round it off a little." She spoke gently, having some idea he must be drunk.

But Rolandsen was not drunk at all; he was sober. He had been working hard of late; the gathering of strangers in the place had kept the telegraph busy.

"No, don't stop yet," he urged. "Cut it round once more—once or twice more—yes, do."

Olga laughed.

"Oh, there's no sense in that!"

"Oh, but your eyes are like twin stars," he said. "And when you smile, it's sunlight all round and all over me."

She took away the cloth, and brushed him down, and swept up the hair from the floor. Rolandsen bent down to help her, and their hands met. She was a maid, he felt the breath of her lips close to, and it thrilled him warmly. He took her hand. Her dress, he saw, was fastened at the throat with just an ordinary pin. It looked wretchedly poor.

"Oh—what did you do that for?" she stammered.

"Nothing. I mean, thank you for doing my hair. If it wasn't for being firmly and everlastingly promised to another, I'd be in love with you this minute."

She stood up with the clippings of hair in her hands, and he leaned back.

"Now your clothes'll be all in a mess," she said, and left the room.

When her father came in, Rolandsen had to be jovial once more; he stretched out his shorn head, and drew his hat down over his ears to show it was too big for him now. Then suddenly he looked at the time, said he must get back to the station, and went off.

Rolandsen went to the store. He asked to look at some brooches and pins—the most expensive sort. He picked out an imitation cameo, and said he would pay for it later, if that would do. But that would not do; Rolandsen owed too much already. Consequently, he was reduced to taking a cheap little glass thing, coloured to look like agate—this being all his few small coins would run to. And Rolandsen went off with his treasure.

That was the evening before....

And now, here sits Rolandsen in his room, and cannot get on with his work. He puts on his hat and goes out to see who it might be waving branches in the wood. And walks straight into the lion's jaws. Jomfru van Loos it was had made that sign, and she stands there waiting for him. Better have curbed his curiosity.

"*Goddag!*" says Jomfru van Loos. "What on earth have you been doing with your hair?"

"I always have it cut in the spring," said he.

"I cut it for you last year. I wasn't good enough this, it seems."

"I'm not going to have any quarrels with you," says he.

"Oh, aren't you?"

"No, I'm not. And you've no call to stand here pulling up all the forest by the roots for everyone to see."

"You've no call to stand there being funny," says she.

"Why don't you stand out down on the road and wave an olive branch?" says Rolandsen.

"Did you cut your hair yourself?"

"Olga cut my hair, if you want to know."

Yes, Olga, who might one day be the wife of Frederik Mack; she had cut his hair. Rolandsen was not inclined to hide the fact; on the contrary, it was a thing to be blazoned abroad.

"Olga, did you say?"

"Well, and why not? Her father couldn't."

"I'm tired of your goings-on," said Jomfru van Loos. "Don't

you be surprised if you find it's all over between us one fine day."

Rolandsen stood thinking for a moment.

"Why, perhaps that would be best," he said.

"What!" cried Jomfru van Loos. "What's that you say?"

"I say you're clean out of your senses in the spring. Look at me now; did you ever see the least little restlessness about me in the spring?"

"Oh, you're a man," she answered carelessly. "But, anyhow, I won't put up with this nonsense about Olga."

"This new priest—is he rich?" asked Rolandsen.

Jomfru van Loos wiped her eyes and turned sharp and sensible all at once.

"Rich? As far as I can see he's as poor as can be."

Rolandsen's hope was shattered.

"You should see his clothes," she went on. "And her's. Why, some of her petticoats.... But he's a wonderful preacher. Have you heard him?"

"No."

"One of the wonderfullest preachers I've ever heard," says Jomfru van Loos in her Bergen dialect.

"And you're quite sure he's not rich?"

"I know this much; he's been up to the store, and asked them to let him have things on credit from there."

For a moment Rolandsen's world was darkened, and he turned to go.

"Are you going?" asked Jomfru van Loos.

"Why, yes. What did you want with me, anyway?"

So that was the way he took it! Well, now ... Jomfru van Loos was already some way converted by the new priest, and strove to be meek and mild, but her nature would break out now and again.

"You mark my words," she said. "You're going too far."

"All right!" said Rolandsen.

"You're doing me a cruel wrong."

"Maybe," said Rolandsen coolly as ever.

"I can't bear it any longer; I'll have to give you up."

Rolandsen thought this over once more. And then he said:

"I thought it would come to this. But seeing I'm not God, I can't help it. Do as you please."

"Right, then," said she furiously.

"That first evening up here in the wood—you weren't in such a temper then. I kissed you, and never a sound you made then but the loveliest little squeak."

"I *didn't* squeak," said Jomfru van Loos indignantly.

"And I loved you for ever and ever, and thought you were going to be a fine particular joy. Ho, indeed!"

"Never you mind about me," she said bitterly. "But what's it to come to with you now?"

"Me? Oh, I don't know. I don't care now, anyway."

"For you needn't imagine it'll ever come to anything with you and Olga. She's to have Frederik Mack."

Was she? thought Rolandsen. So it was common talk already. He walked away thoughtfully, and Jomfru van Loos went with him. They came down on to the road and walked on.

"You look nice with your hair short," she said. "But it's badly cut, wretchedly badly cut."

"Can you lend me three hundred *Daler*?" he asked.

"Three hundred *Daler*?"

"For six months."

"I wouldn't lend you the money anyway. It's all over between us now."

Rolandsen nodded, and said, "Right, then, that's agreed."

But when they reached the Vicarage gate, where Rolandsen

had to turn off, she said, "I haven't the money. I wish I had."
She gave him her hand, and said, "I can't stand here any longer
now; good-bye for the present." And when she had gone a few
steps, she turned round and said, "Isn't there anything else
you'd like me to say?"

"No; what should there be?" said Rolandsen. "I've nothing
that I know of."

She went. And Rolandsen felt a sense of relief, and hoped in
his heart it might be for the last time.

There was a bill stuck up on the fence, and he stopped to
read it; it was Trader Mack's latest announcement about the
burglary: Four hundred *Speciedaler* for information. The
reward would be paid even to the thief himself if he came
forward and confessed.

Four hundred *Speciedaler*! thought Rolandsen to himself.

V

No, the new priest was not a rich man, far from it. It was only his poor little wife who was full of thoughtless, luxurious fancies she had been brought up with, and wanted a host of servants and such. There was nothing for her to do herself in the house; they had no children, and she had never learned housekeeping, and that was why she was for ever hatching childish ideas out of her little head. A sweet and lovely torment in the house she was.

Heavens alive, how the good priest had fought his comical battles with his wife again and again, trying to teach her a scrap of sense and thought and order! For four years he had striven with her in vain. He picked up threads and bits of paper from the floor, put odds and ends of things in their proper places, closed the door after her, tended the stoves, and screwed the ventilators as was needed. When his wife went out, he would make a tour of the rooms and see the state she had left them in: hairpins here, there, and everywhere; combs full of combings; handkerchiefs lying about; chairs piled up with garments. And he shuddered and put things straight again. In his bachelor days, when he lived by himself in an attic, he had felt less homeless than he did now.

He had scolded and entreated at first, with some effect; his wife admitted he was right, and promised to improve. And then she would get up early the next morning and set about putting things in order high and low, like a child in a sudden fit of earnestness, playing "grown-up peoples," and overdoing it. But the fit never lasted; a few days after all was as before. It never occurred to her to wonder at the disorder when it appeared once more; on the contrary, she could not understand why her husband should begin again with his constant discontent. "I knocked over that dish and it smashed," she would say. "It was only a cheap thing, so it doesn't matter."—"But the pieces have been lying about ever since this morning," he answered.

One day she came in and told him that Oline the maid would have to go. Oline the maid had been rude enough to complain about her mistress's way of taking things out of the kitchen and leaving them about all over the place.

And so, after a time, the priest grew hardened to it all, and gave up his daily protest; he still went on setting in order and putting things straight, but it was with compressed lips and as few words as might be. And his wife made no remark; she was used to having someone to clear up after her. Her husband, indeed, really felt at times that she was to be pitied. There she was, going about so pleasantly, a trifle thin, and poorly dressed, yet never uttering a sigh at her poverty, though she had been brought up to lack for nothing. She would sit and sew, altering her dresses that had been altered so many times already, humming over her work as cheerfully as a young girl. Then suddenly her childishness would break out; the mistress of the house would throw down her work, leave everything strewed as it fell, and go off for a walk. And chairs and tables might be left for days strewn with tacked sleeves and unpicked skirts. Where did she go? It was an old habit of hers from her youth at home to go fluttering about among the shops; she delighted in buying things. She could always find some use for remnants of material, bits of ribbon, combs and perfumes and toilet trifles, odd little metal things, matchboxes, and the like. Much better buy a big thing and have done with it, thought her husband; never mind if it were expensive and brought him into debt.

He might try to write a book, a popular Church history, or something, and pay for it that way.

And so the years passed. There were frequent little quarrels; but the two were fond of each other none the less, and as long as the priest did not interfere too much, they managed well enough. But he had a troublesome way of keeping an eye on some little thing or other even from a distance, even from his office window; only yesterday he had noticed a couple of blankets left out in the rain. Should he tell someone? Then suddenly he saw his wife coming back from her walk, hurrying in out of the rain. She would notice them herself, no doubt. But she went straight up to her room. He called out into the kitchen; there was no one there, and he could hear Jomfru van Loos out in the dairy. So he went out himself and brought the blankets in.

And so the matter might have passed off, and no more said. But the priest could not keep his peace, foolish man. In the evening his wife asked for the blankets. They were brought. "They're wet," said she.—"They would have been wetter if I hadn't fetched them in out of the rain," said her husband. But at that she turned on him. "Was it you that fetched them in? There was no need for you to do anything of the sort; I would have told the maids myself to fetch them in." He smiled bitterly at that; if he had left it till she told the maids, the blankets would have been hanging out now.

But his wife was offended. Was there any need to make such a fuss about a drop of rain or so? "Oh, but you're unreasonable," she said; "always bothering about all sorts of things."—"I wish I were not obliged to bother about such things," said he. "Just look at your washing-basin now; what's it doing on the bed?"— "I put it there because there was no room anywhere else."—"If you had another wash-stand, it would be all the same," said he. "You'd have that loaded up with other things too in no time." Then she lost patience, and said, "Oh, how can you be so unreasonable; really, I think you must be ill. I can't bear any more of it, I can't!" And she sat down, staring before her.

But she bore it all the same. A moment after it was all forgotten, and her kind heart forgave him the wrong. Careless and happy she was; it was her nature.

And the priest kept more and more to his study, where the general disorder of the house rarely penetrated. He was a big, sturdy man, and worked like a horse. He had inquired of his lay-helpers as to the moral tone of the village, and what he learned was by no means satisfactory. Wherefore he wrote letters of reprimand and warning to one and another of his flock, and where that did not avail, he went in person to visit the delinquents, till he came to be looked on with respect and awe. He spared none. He had himself ascertained that one of his helpers, Levion, had a sister who was far too easy and accommodating towards the fisher-lads; she too received a letter. He sent for her brother, and gave him the letter to deliver. "Give her that. And tell her I shall watch her goings about with an observant eye!"

Trader Mack came to call one day, and was shown into the parlour. It was a brief but important visit. Mack came to offer his assistance if any should be needed in helping the poor of the village. The priest thanked him, glad at heart. If he had not been sure of it before, at least he knew now, that Mack of Rosengaard was the protector of them all. An elegant, authoritative old gentleman; even Fruen herself, town-bred as she was, could not but feel impressed. A great man, beyond doubt—and those must be real stones in the pin he wore in his shirt-front.

"The fishery's doing well," said Mack. "I've made another haul. Nothing to speak of, only some twenty barrels, but it all helps, you know. And then it occurred to me that we ought not to forget our duty towards our neighbours."

"Just so!" said the priest delightedly. "That's as it should be. And twenty barrels, is that what you would call a little haul? I've no knowledge of these matters myself."

"Well, two or three thousand barrels would be better."

"Two or three thousand!" said Fruen. "Only fancy!"

"But when I don't make big enough hauls myself, I can always buy from others. There was a boat from the outlying parts made a good haul yesterday; I bought it up on the spot. I'm going to load every vessel I've got with herring."

"It's a big business this of yours," said the priest.

Mack admitted that it was getting on that way. It was an old-established business when he came into it, he said, but he had worked it up, and extended its operations. For the sake of the children, he felt he must.

"But, heavens, how many factories and stores and things have you altogether?" asked Fruen enthusiastically.

Mack laughed, and said, "Really, *Frue*, I couldn't say offhand, without counting."

But Mack forgot his troubles and annoyances for a little as he sat talking; he was by no means displeased at being asked about his numerous factories and stores.

"You've a bakery at Rosengaard," said Fruen, thinking all at once of her housekeeping. "I wish we lived nearer. We can't make nice bread, somehow, at home here."

"There's a baker at the *Lensmandsgaard.*"

"Yes, but he's never any bread."

"He drinks a great deal, I'm sorry to say," put in the priest. "I've written him a letter, but for all that...."

Mack was silent a moment. "I'll set up a bakery here, then," he said. "Seeing there's a branch of the store already."

Mack was almighty; he could do whatever he willed. But a word from him, and lo, a bakery on the spot!

"Only think of it!" cried Fruen, and looked at him with wondering eyes.

"You shall have your bread all right, *Frue*. I'll telegraph at once for the men to come down. It'll take a little time, perhaps—a few weeks, no more."

But the priest said nothing. What if his housekeeper and all the maids baked the bread that was needed? Bread would be dearer now.

"I have to thank you for kindly allowing me credit at the store," said the priest.

"Yes," put in his wife, and was thoughtful once more.

"Not at all," said Mack. "Most natural thing in the world. Anything you want—it's at your service."

"It must be wonderful to have such power," says Fruen.

"I've not as much power as I could wish," says Mack. "There's that burglary, for instance. I can't find out who did it."

"It was really too bad, that business," broke in the priest. "I see you have offered a heavy reward, even to the thief himself, and still he won't confess."

Mack shook his head.

"Oh, but it's the blackest ingratitude to steal from you," says Fruen.

Mack took up the cue. "Since you mention it, *Frue*, I will say I had not expected it. No, indeed, I had not. I have not treated my people so badly as to deserve it."

Here the priest put in, "A thief will steal where there is most to steal. And in this case he knew where to go."

The priest, in all innocence, had found the very word. Mack felt easier at once. Putting it like that made the whole thing less of a disgrace to himself.

"But people are talking," he said. "Saying all sorts of things. It hurts my feelings, and might even do serious harm. There are a number of strangers here just now, and they are none too careful of their words. And my daughter Elise feels it very deeply. Well," he said, rising to his feet, "it will pass off in time, no doubt. And, as I was saying, if you come across any deserving case in the village, remember I shall be most pleased to help."

Mack took his leave. He had formed an excellent impression of the priest and his wife, and would put in a good word for them wherever he could. It would do them no harm. Though perhaps.... Who could say to what lengths the gossip about himself had reached already? Only yesterday his son Frederik had come home and told how a drunken seaman had called to him from a boat, "Hey, when are you going to give yourself up and get the reward?"

VI

The days were getting warmer now; the catches of herring had to be left in the nets for fear of spoiling, and could only be turned out in the cool of the night, or when it rained. And there was no fishing now to speak of anyway, being already too late in the season; one or two of the stranger boats had left. And there was field-work to be done, and need of all hands at home.

The nights too were brilliant and full of sun. It was weather for dreams; for little fluttering quests of the heart. Young folk walked the roads by night, singing and waving branches of willow. And from every rocky islet came the calling of birds—of loon and gull and eider-duck. And the seal thrust up its dripping head from the water, looked round, and dived again down to its own world below. Ove Rolandsen too felt the spell; now and again he could be heard singing or strumming in his room of nights, and that was more than need be looked for from a man who was no longer a youth. And, indeed, it was not for any meaningless delight he twanged and trolled his songs, but rather by way of diversion, by way of relief from his weighty thoughts. Rolandsen is thinking deeply these days; he is in a quandary, and must find a way out. Jomfru van Loos, of course, had turned up again; she was not given to extravagant wastefulness in matters of love, and she held now by their betrothal as before. On the other hand, Ove Rolandsen, as he had said, was not God; he could not keep that heart of his within bounds in spring. It was hard on a man to have a betrothed who would not understand when matters were clearly broken off between them.

Rolandsen had been down to visit the parish clerk again, and there was Olga sitting outside the door. But there was a deal of money about just now, with herring at six *Ort* the barrel, and Olga seemed inclined to put on airs. Or what else could it be? Was he, Rolandsen, the sort of man a girl could afford to pass by? She merely glanced up at him, and went on with her knitting as before.

Said Rolandsen, "There! You looked up. Your eyes are like arrows; they wound a man."

"I don't understand you," said Olga.

"Oh! And do you suppose I understand myself? Not in the least. I've lost my senses. Here I am now, for instance, paving the way for you to plague me through the night that's to come."

"Then why don't you go away?" said Olga.

"I was listening to a voice last night—a voice within me. All unspeakable things it said. In a word, I resolved to take a great decision, if you think you can advise me to do it."

"How can I? I've nothing to do with it."

"Ho!" said Rolandsen. "You're full of bitter words to-day. Sitting there lashing out all the time. Talking of something else, you'll have that hair of yours falling off before long. There's too much of it."

Olga was silent.

"Do you know Børre the organ-blower? There's a girl of his I could have if I cared."

Olga burst out laughing at that, and stared at him.

"For Heaven's sake don't sit there smiling like that. It only makes me wilder than ever in love."

"Oh, you're quite mad," says Olga softly, flushing red.

"Sometimes I think to myself: perhaps she laughs up at me that way just to make me lose my senses all the more. That's how they kill ducks and geese, you know, jab them a little in the head with a knife, and then they swell, and it makes them all the finer."

Olga answered offendedly, "I don't do anything of the sort; you need not think so." And she rose, and made as if to go indoors.

"If you go now," said Rolandsen, "I shall only come in after you, and ask your father if he's read the books."

"Father's not at home."

"Well, I didn't come to see him, anyway. But you, Olga, you're bitter and unapproachable this day. There's no wringing a drop of kindness out of you. You never heed me, you pass me by."

Olga laughed again.

"But there's that girl of Børre's," said Rolandsen. "Her name's Pernille. I've heard them call her so myself. And her father blows the organ at church."

"Must you have a sweetheart dangling at every finger?" asked Olga seriously.

"Marie van Loos is my betrothed," he answered. "But it's all over between us now. Ask her yourself. I expect she'll be going away soon."

"Yes, mother, I'm coming," called Olga in through the window.

"Your mother wasn't calling you at all; she only looked at you."

"Yes, but I know what she meant."

"Oh, very well then! I'll go. But look you, Olga, you know what I mean too, only you don't answer me the same way, and say, Yes, I'm coming."

She opened the door. Rolandsen felt he had abased himself; she would not think of him now as the lordly man he was. He must raise himself once more in her esteem. It would never do to show himself so utterly defeated. So he began talking of death, and was highly humorous about it; now he would have to die, and he didn't care much if he did. But he had his own ideas about the funeral. He would make a bell himself to ring his knell, and the clapper should be fashioned from the thighbone of an ox, because he had been such a fool in life. And the funeral oration was to be the shortest ever known; the priest to set his foot upon the grave and simply say, "I hereby declare you mortified, null, and void!"

But Olga was getting weary of all this, and had lost her shyness now. Moreover, she had a red ribbon at her throat, like any lady, and the pin was altogether hidden.

"I must make her look up to me properly," thought Rolandsen. And he said, "Now I did think something would come of this. My former sweetheart, Marie van Loos, she's broidered and worked me all over with initials till I'm a wonder to see; there's Olga Rolandsen, or what's all but the same, on every stitch of my things. And I took it as a sign from Heaven. But I must be going. My best respects...."

And Rolandsen waved his hat and walked off, ending on a lordly note. Surely, after that, it would be strange if she did not think and wonder over him a little now.

What was it that had happened? Even the parish clerk's daughter had refused him. Well and good! But was there not much to indicate that it was all a sham? Why had she been sitting outside the door at all if it were not that she had seen him coming? And why had she decked herself out with red ribbons like a lady?

But, a few evenings later, Rolandsen's conceit was shattered. From his window he saw Olga go down to Mack's store. She stayed there till quite late, and when she went home, Frederik Mack and his sister Elise walked up with her. And here, of course, the lordly Rolandsen should have kept calm, and merely hummed a little tune, or drummed with his fingers carelessly, and kept his thoughts on his work. Instead of which, he snatched up his hat and made off at once towards the woods. He hurried round in a wide curve, and came out on the road far ahead of the three. Then he stopped to get his breath, and walked down to meet them.

But the three took an unreasonable time; Rolandsen could neither hear nor see them. He whistled and trolled a bit of a song, as if they might sit somewhere in the woods and watch him. At last he saw them coming, walking slowly, dawdling unpardonably, seeing it was late at night, and they should have been hurrying towards their respective homes. Rolandsen, great man, walks towards them, with a long stalk of grass in his mouth and a sprig of willow in his buttonhole; the two men raised their hats as they came up, and the ladies nodded.

"You look warm," said Frederik. "Where have you been?"

Rolandsen answered over his shoulder, "It's spring-time; I'm walking in the spring."

No nonsense this time, but clean firmness and confidence. Ho! but he had walked past them with an air—slowly, carelessly, all unperturbed; he had even found strength to measure Elise Mack with a downward glance. But no sooner had they passed out of sight than he slipped aside into the wood, no longer great at all, but abject. Olga was a creature of no importance now; and at the thought of it, he took the agate pin from his pocket, broke it up thoroughly, and threw it away. But now there was Elise, Mack's daughter Elise, tall and brown, and showing her white teeth a little when she smiled. Elise it was whom God had led across his path. She had not said a word, and to-morrow, perhaps, she would be going away again. All hope gone.

Well and good....

But on coming back to the telegraph station, there was Jomfru van Loos waiting for him. Once before he had reminded her that past was past, and what was done was over; she had much better go away and live somewhere else. And Jomfru van Loos had answered that he should not have to ask her twice—good-bye! But now here she was again, waiting for him.

"Here's that tobacco pouch I promised you," she said. "Here it is, if you're not too proud."

He did not take it, but answered, "A tobacco pouch? I never use that sort of thing."

"Oh, is that so?" said she, and drew back her hand.

And he forced himself to soften her again. "It can't be me you promised it. Think again; perhaps it was the priest. And he's a married man."

She did not understand that the slight jest had cost him some effort, and she could not refrain from answering in turn, "I saw the ladies up along the road; I suppose that's where you've been, trailing after them?"

"And what's that to do with you?"

"Ove!"

"Why don't you go away somewhere else? You can see for yourself it's no good going on like this."

"It would be all right as ever, if only you weren't such a jewel to go flaunting about with all the womenfolk."

"Do you want to drive me out of my wits?" he cried. "Good-night!"

Jomfru van Loos called after him, "Ho, yes, you are a nice one, indeed! There's this and that I've heard about you!"

Now was there any sense at all in being so desperately particular? And couldn't a poor soul have a little genuine heartache to bear with into the bargain? The end of it was, that Rolandsen went into the office, straight to the instrument, called up the station at Rosengaard, and asked his colleague there to send him half a keg of cognac with the next consignment coming down. There was no sense in going on like this for ever.

VII

Elise Mack stays some little while at the factory this time. She has left the big house at Rosengaard and come out here wholly and solely to make things a little comfortable for her father during his stay. She would hardly set her foot in the village at all if she could avoid it.

Elise Mack was growing more and more of a fine lady; she wore red and white and yellow gowns, and people were beginning to call her *Frøken*, though her father was neither priest nor doctor. A sun and a star she was above all others.

She came to the station with some telegrams to be sent; Rolandsen received her. He said nothing beyond the few words needed, and did not make the mistake of nodding as to an acquaintance and asking how she was. Not a single mistake did he make.

"It says 'ostrich feathers' twice in this. I don't know if it's meant to be that way."

"Twice?" said she. "Let me look. Oh no, of course not; you're quite right. Lend me a pen, would you mind?"

She took off her glove, and went on speaking as she wrote. "And that's to a merchant in town; he'd have laughed at me ever so. There, it's all right now, isn't it?"

"Quite right now."

"And so you're still here?" she said, keeping her seat. "Year after year and I find you here."

Rolandsen had his reasons, no doubt, for staying on at this little station instead of applying for a better post. There must be something that held him to the place, year after year.

"Must be somewhere," he answered.

"You might come to Rosengaard. That's better than here, surely?"

The faintest little blush spread over her cheeks as she spoke; perhaps she would rather have left that unsaid.

"They wouldn't give me a big station like that."

"Well, now, I suppose you are rather too young."

"It is kind of you, anyhow, to think it's because of that."

"If you came over to us, now, there's more society. The Doctor's next door, and the cashier, and all the assistants from the store. And there are always some queer people coming in— sea-captains, you know, and that sort."

"Captain Henriksen of the coasting steamer," thought Rolandsen to himself.

But what was the meaning of all this graciousness coming so suddenly? Was Rolandsen another man to-day than yesterday? He knew well enough that he was utterly and entirely hopeless in this foolish love of his; there was no more to be said. She gave him her hand as she rose to go, and that without first putting on her glove. There was a rustle of silk as she swept down the steps.

Rolandsen drew up to the table, a threadbare, stooping figure, and sent off the wires. His breast was a whirl of strange feelings. All things considered, he was not so desperately off after all; the invention might bring in a heavy sum if only he could first get hold of three hundred *Daler*. He was a bankrupt millionaire. But surely he must be able to find some way....

The *Præstefruen* came in, with a telegram to her people. Rolandsen had gathered courage from the previous visit. He no longer felt himself as an insignificant next-to-nothing, but the equal of other great men; he talked to Fruen a little, just a word or so in the ordinary way. And Fruen, on her part, stayed somewhat longer than was strictly necessary, and asked him to look in at the Vicarage any time.

That evening he met her again, Fruen herself, on the road just below the station. And she did not hurry away, but stayed talking a little while. It could hardly be displeasing to her, since she stayed so.

"You play the guitar, I think," she said.

"Yes. If you like to wait a little, I'll show you how well I can play."

And he went inside to fetch his guitar.

Fruen waited. It could not be altogether displeasing to her, since she waited so.

And Rolandsen sang for her, of his true love and his heart's delight; and the songs were nothing wonderful, but his voice was fine and full. Rolandsen had a purpose of his own in thus keeping her there in the middle of the road; there was every chance that someone might come walking by about that time. Such things had happened before. And if Fruen had been pressed for time, it would have been awkward for her now; they fell to talking again, and stayed talking some time. This Rolandsen spoke in a way of his own, altogether different from her husband's manner, as if it were from some other part of the world. And when he rolled out his most magnificent phrases, her eyes rounded wide as those of a listening child.

"Well, God be with you"* she said at last, turning to go.

"So He is, I'm sure," answered Rolandsen.

She started. "Are you sure of that? How?"

"Well, He's every reason to be. He's Lord of all creation, I know, but I shouldn't think there's anything much in being just a God of beasts and mountains. After all, it's us human beings that make Him what He is. So why shouldn't He be with us?"

And, having delivered himself of this striking speech,

* _Gud vare med Dem._ The expression is often used, with no more special significance than our own abbreviation of the same words in "Good-bye." But Rolandsen here chooses to take it literally.

Rolandsen looked extremely pleased with himself. Fruen wondered at him greatly as she walked away. Ho-ho! 'Twas not for nothing that the knob of a head he bore on his shoulders had devised a great invention.

But now the cognac had come. Rolandsen had carried the keg up from the wharf himself; he went no back-ways round with his burden, but carried it openly under his powerful arm in broad daylight. So unafraid was he at heart. And then came a time when Rolandsen found comfort for all distress. And there were nights when he turned out and made himself regent and master of all roads and ways; he cleared them bare, and made them impassable for stranger men from the boats, coming ashore on their lawful errands, in search of petticoats.

One Sunday a boat's crew appeared at church, all reasonably drunk. After the service they sauntered up and down the road, instead of going on board; they had a supply of *Brændevin* with them, and drank themselves ever more boisterous, to the annoyance of those passing by. The priest himself had come up to reprove them, but without effect; later, the *Lensmand* himself came up, and he wore a gold-laced cap. Some of them went on board after that, but three of them—Big Ulrik was one—refused to budge. They had come ashore, they said, and were going to let folk know it; as for the girls, they were their girls for now. Ulrik was with them, and Ulrik was a man well known from Lofoten to Finmarken. Come on then!

A number of people from the village had gathered about, farther off along the road, or in among the trees, as their courage permitted. They glanced with some concern at Big Ulrik swaggering about.

"I must ask you men to go on board again," said the *Lensmand*. "If you don't, I'll have to talk to you after another fashion."

"Go along home, you and your cap," said Ulrik.

The *Lensmand* was thinking already of getting help, and tying up the madman out of harm's way.

"And you'd better be careful how you defy me when I'm in uniform," says the *Lensmand*.

Ulrik and his fellows laughed at this till they had to hold their ribs. A fisher-lad ventured boldly past; one of them struck him a *Skalle*,[†] and drew blood. "Now for the next," cried Ulrik.

"A rope," cried the *Lensmand*, at sight of the blood. "Bring a rope, some of you, and help me take him."

"How many are there of you?" asked Ulrik the invincible. And the three doughty ones laughed and gasped again.

But now came Big Rolandsen up along the road, walking with a soft, gliding step, and his eyes staring stiffly. He was on his usual round. He greeted the *Lensmand*, and stopped.

"Here's Rolandsen," cried Ulrik. "Ho, boys, look at him!"

"He's dangerous," said the *Lensmand*. "He's drawn blood from one already. We shall have to rope him."

"Rope him?"

The *Lensmand* nodded. "Yes. I won't stand any more of this."

"Nonsense," said Rolandsen. "What do you want with a rope? You leave me to tackle him."

Ulrik stepped closer, made pretence to lift his hand in greeting, and gave Rolandsen a slight blow. He felt, no doubt, that he had struck something firm and solid, for he drew back, but kept on shouting defiantly, "Goddag, Telegraph-Rolandsen! And there's your name and titles for all to hear."

After that, it seemed as if nothing would happen. Rolandsen was not inclined to let slip the chance of a fight, and it annoyed him that he was so miserably slow to anger, and had not returned the first blow. He had to begin now by answering the other's taunts, in order to keep matters going. They fooled about a little, talking drunken-fashion, and each boasting of

---

† A blow delivered with the head, hitting downward or sideways at an opponent's face.

what he would do to the other. When one invited the other to come on, and he would give him a dose of olive oil enough to last him, etcetera, the other answered, right, he would come on sure enough as soon as anyone else did, and provide sufficient laying on of hands by return. And the crowd around them found these interchanges creditable to both sides. But the *Lensmand*, watching, could see how wrath was growing and flourishing up in Rolandsen's mind; Rolandsen was smiling all the time as he talked.

Then Ulrik flicked him under the nose, and at that Rolandsen was in the proper mood at once; he shot out one swift hand and gripped the other's coat. But the stuff gave way, and there was nothing very grand in ripping up a duffle jacket. Rolandsen made a spring forward, showing his teeth in a satisfied grimace. And then things began to happen.

Ulrik tried a *Skalle*, and Rolandsen was thenceforward aware of his opponent's speciality. But Rolandsen was past-master in another effective method—the long, swinging, flat-handed cut delivered edgeways at the jawbone; the blow should fall just on the side of the chin. A blow of this sort shakes up a man most adequately; his head whirls, and down he comes with a crash. It breaks no bones, and draws no blood save for a tiny trickle from the nose and mouth. The stricken one is in no hurry to move.

Suddenly Big Ulrik has it, and down he comes, staggering and falling beyond the edge of the road. His legs tangled crosswise under him and collapsed as if dead; faintness overpowered him. And Rolandsen was well enough up in the slang of the brawl. "Now for the next," he said at once. He seemed thoroughly pleased with himself, and never heeded that his shirt was torn open at the throat.

But the next one was two, being Ulrik's fellow-rascals both;

quiet and wondering they were now, and no longer holding their ribs in an ache of laughter.

"You! You're children," cried Rolandsen to the pair. "But if you want to be crumpled up...."

The *Lensmand* intervened, and talked the two disturbers to their senses; they had better pick up their comrade and help him on board then and there. "I'm in your debt," he said to Rolandsen.

But Rolandsen, watching the three desperadoes as they moved off down the road, was far from satisfied yet. He shouted after them as long as they could hear, "Come again to-morrow! Smash a window down at the station and I'll know. Huh! Children!"

As usual he did not know when to stop, but went on with his boastful talk. But the crowd was moving away. Suddenly a lady comes up, looks at him with glistening eyes, and offers her hand. *Præstefruen* and no other. She too has seen the fight.

"Oh, it was splendid!" she says. "I'm sure he won't forget it in a hurry."

She noticed that his shirt was open. The sun had browned a ring about his neck, but he was naked and white below.

He pulls his shirt together and bows. It was by no means unwelcome to be accosted thus by the chaplain's lady in sight of all; the victor of that battle feels himself elated, he can afford to speak kindly for a moment to this slip of a child that she is. Poor lady, her shoes were none too impressive, and it was but little homage or deference any paid to her there!

"'Tis misusing such eyes to trouble them looking at me," said he.

Whereat she blushed.

He asked her again, "Don't you miss things, living away from town?"

"Oh no," she answered. "It's nice living here too. But look here, wouldn't you care to walk up and spend the day with us now?"

Rolandsen thanked her, and was sorry he could not. Sunday or Monday, it was all one to the telegraph station. "But I thank you all the same," he said. "There's one thing I envy the priest, and that is you."

"What do you...?"

"Politely, but firmly, I envy him his wife."

There—he had done it now. Surely it would be hard to find the like of Ove Rolandsen for shedding little joys abroad.

"What ridiculous things you do say," said Fruen, when she had recovered herself a little.

But Rolandsen, walking back homeward, reflected that, taking it all round, he had had a nice day. In his intoxication and triumph he dwelt on the fact that this young wife, the priest's wife, was so inclined to stop and talk with him at times. He formed his own ideas about it, and grew cunning, ay, he began already to plot and plan. Why should not Fruen herself get rid of Jomfru van Loos for him, and file through his fetters? He could not ask it of her directly, no—but there were other ways. Who could say? Perhaps she would do him that service, since they were such good friends.

VIII

The priest and his lady are awakened in the night; wakened by song. No such thing had ever happened to them before, but here it was; somebody singing outside the house down below. The sun looks out over the world; the gulls are awake; it is three in the morning.

"Surely there's someone singing," says the priest to his wife in the adjoining room.

"Yes, it's here, outside my window," says she.

Fruen listened. She knew the voice—wild Rolandsen's voice it was, and his guitar. Oh, but it was too bad of him really, to come singing of his "true love" right underneath her window. She felt hot all over.

Her husband came in to look. "It's that man Rolandsen," he said, and frowned. "He's had a keg of brandy sent just lately. Disgraceful!"

But Fruen was not inclined to frown upon this little diversion; he was quite a nice young fellow really, this Rolandsen, who could fight like any rough, and sing like a youth inspired. He brought a touch of mild excitement into the quiet, everyday life of the place.

"It's meant to be a serenade, I suppose," she said, with a laugh.

"He's no business to be serenading you," said her husband. "I don't know what you think of it yourself?"

Oh, but of course he must be nasty about it! "There's no harm in it, surely," said his wife. "It's only his fun." But at the same time she resolved never again to make beautiful eyes at Rolandsen and lead him on to escapades of this sort.

"He's beginning again, as sure as I'm here," cried the priest. And he stepped forward to the window then and there, and rapped on the pane.

Rolandsen looked up. It was the priest himself standing there in the flesh. The song died away. Rolandsen collapsed, stood a moment hesitating, and walked away.

"Ah!" said the priest. "I soon got rid of him." He was by no means displeased to have accomplished so much by merely showing himself. "And he shall have a letter from me to-morrow," he went on. "I've had my eye on him for some time past, for his scandalous goings-on."

"Don't you think if I spoke to him myself," said his wife, "and told him not to come up here singing songs in the middle of the night?"

But the priest went on without heeding. "Write him a letter, yes.... And then I'll go and talk to him after." As if his going and talking to Rolandsen after meant something very serious indeed.

He went back to his own room, and lay thinking it all over. No, he would endure it no longer; the fellow's conceit, and his extravagant ways, were becoming a nuisance to the place. The priest was no respecter of persons; he wrote his epistles to one as to another, and made himself feared. If the congregation stumbled in their darkness, it was his business to bring light. He had not forgotten that business with Levion's sister. She had not mended her ways, and the priest had been unable to retain her brother as lay-helper. Ill-fortune had come upon Levion; his wife had died. But the priest lost no time; he spoke to Levion at the funeral. It was an abominable business. Levion, simple soul, setting out to bury his helpmeet, recollected that he had promised to bring up a newly slaughtered calf to Frederik Mack at the factory. It was all on the way, and with the hot weather it would not do to leave the meat over-long. What more natural than that he should take the carcase with him? The priest learned the story from Enok, the humble person with the permanent earache. And he sent for Levion at once.

"I cannot retain you as lay-helper," he said. "Your sister is living a sinful life within your gates; your house is a house of ill-fame; you lie there fast asleep at night and let men come in."

"Ay, more's the pity," says Levion. "I'll not deny it's been that way more than once."

"And there's another thing. You follow your wife to the grave, and drag a dead calf along after her. Now I ask you, is that right or decent?"

But Levion, fisherman-peasant, found such niceties beyond him; he stared uncomprehendingly at the priest. His wife had always been a thrifty soul; she would have been the first to remind him herself to take the calf along if she could have spoken. "Seeing it's up that way," she would have said.

"If as Pastor's going to be so niggling particular," said Levion, "you'll never get a decent helper anywhere."

"That's my business," said the priest. "Anyhow, you are dismissed."

Levion looked down at his sou'wester. It was a blow to him and a disgrace; his neighbours would rejoice at his fall.

But the priest had not finished yet. "For Heaven's sake," he said, "can't you get that sister of yours married to the man?"

"Do you think I haven't tried?" said Levion. "But the worst of it is, she's not quite sure which one it is."

The priest looked at him open-mouthed. "Not quite *what* did you say?" And then at last, realising what it meant, he clasped his hands. "Well, well!... I must find another helper, that is all."

"Who'll it be?"

"That's no concern of yours. As a matter of fact, I am taking

Enok."

Levion stood thoughtful for quite a while. He knew this Enok, and had an old account to settle with him. "Enok, is it?" he said, and went out.

Enok was certainly a good man for the post. He was one of your deep-thinking sort, and did not carry his head in the air, but bowed on his breast; an earnest man. It was whispered that he was no good man to share with in a boat; there was some story of his having been caught, many years back, pulling up other folk's lines. But this, no doubt, was pure envy and malice. There was nothing lordly or baronial about him in the way of looks; that everlasting kerchief round his ears did not improve him. Moreover, he had a way of blowing through his nostrils; on meeting anyone, he would lay a finger first on one side and blow, then on the other side, and blow again. But the Lord took no account of outward things, and Enok, His humble servant, had doubtless no other thought with this beyond smartening himself up a little on meeting with his fellows. When he came up he would say, "*Freden!*" and when he went away, "*Bliv i Freden.*"* Sound and thoughtful, an earnest man. Even his *tollekniv*, the big knife at his belt, he seemed to wear with thankfulness, as who should say, "Alas, there's many that haven't so much as a knife to cut with in the world." Only last Offering, Enok had created a sensation by the amount of his gift; he had laid a note on the altar. Had he been doing so well of late in ready cash? Doubtless some higher power must have added its mite to his savings. He owed nothing in Mack's books at the store; his fish-loft was untouched, his family were decently clad. And Enok ruled his house with strictness and propriety. He had a son, a very model of quiet and decorous behaviour. The lad had been out with the fishing fleet from Lofoten, and earned the right to come home with a blue anchor on his hand, but this he did not.

* "Peace" and "Be in Peace." These are more rustic forms of greeting than the "*Goddag*" and "*Farvel*" generally used.

His father had instructed him early in humility and the fear of God. It was a blessed thing, in Enok's mind, to walk humbly and meekly....

The priest lay thinking over these things, and the morning wore on. That miserable Rolandsen had spoiled his night's rest; he got up at six, which was all too early. But then it appeared that his wife had already dressed and gone out without a sound.

During the forenoon Fruen walked in to Rolandsen and said, "You must not come up like that and sing songs outside at night."

"I know; it was wrong of me," he said. "I thought Jomfru van Loos would be there, but she had moved."

"Oh!... So it was for her you sang?"

"Yes. A poor little bit of a song to greet the day."

"That was my room," said she.

"It used to be Jomfruen's room in the old priest's time."

Fruen said no more; her eyes had turned dull and stupid.

"Well, thanks," she said, as she went. "It was very nice, I'm sure, but don't do it again."

"I won't, I promise.... If I'd known ... of course, I wouldn't have dared...." Rolandsen looked utterly crushed.

When Fruen came home she said, "Really I'm so sleepy to-day."

"No wonder," said her husband. "You got no sleep last night, with that fellow shouting down there."

"I think Jomfru van Loos had better go," said she.

"Jomfru van Loos?"

"He's engaged to her, you know. And we shall have no peace at night."

"I'll send him a letter to-day!"

"Wouldn't it be simpler just to send her away?"

The priest thought to himself that this was by no means the

simplest way, seeing it would mean further expense for a new housekeeper. Moreover, Jomfru van Loos was very useful; without her, there would be no sort of order anywhere. He remembered how things had been managed at first, when his wife looked after the house herself—he was not likely to forget it.

"Whom will you get in her place?" he asked.

"I would rather do her work myself," she answered.

At that he laughed bitterly, and said, "A nice mess you will make of it."

But his wife was hurt and offended at this. "I can't see," she said, "but that I must look after the house in any case. So the work a housekeeper did would not make much difference."

The priest was silent. It was no use discussing it further, no earthly use—no. "We can't send her away," he said. But[95] there was his wife with her shoes all sorely cracked and worn, pitiful to see. And he said as he went out, "We must manage to get you a new pair of shoes, and that soon."

"Oh, it's summer now," she answered.

IX

The last of the fishing-boats are ready to sail; the season is over. But the sea was still rich; herring were sighted along the coast, and prices fell. Trader Mack had bought up what fish he could get, and none had heard of any stoppage in his payments; only the last boat he had asked to wait while he telegraphed south for money. But at that folk had begun whispering at once. Mack was in difficulties.... Aha!

But Trader Mack was as all-powerful as ever. In the thick of all his other business he had promised the Vicarage people a bakery. Good! The bakery was getting on, the workmen had arrived, and the foundation was already laid. Fruen found it a real pleasure to go and watch her bakery growing up. But now the building-work was to commence, and this was a matter for other workmen; they had been telegraphed for too, said Mack.

Meantime, however, the baker at the *Lensmandsgaard* had pulled himself together. What a letter from the priest had failed to accomplish, was effected by Mack with his foundation. "If it's bread they want, why, they shall have it," said the baker. But everyone understood that the poor man was only writhing helplessly; he would be crushed now, crushed by Mack.

Rolandsen sits in his room drawing up a curious announcement, with his signature. He reads it over again and again, and approves it. Then he puts it in his pocket, takes his hat, and goes out. He took the road down to Mack's office at the factory.

Rolandsen had been expecting Jomfru van Loos to go away, but she had not gone; her mistress had not dismissed her at all. Rolandsen had been out in his reckoning when he hoped that Fruen would do him favours. He came to his reasonable senses again, and thought to himself, Let's keep to earth now; we haven't made such an impression after all, it seems.

On the other hand, he had received a letter of serious and chastening content from the priest himself. Rolandsen did not attempt to hide the fact that this thing had happened to him; he told the matter to all, to high and low. It was no more than he deserved, he said, and it had done him good; no priest had ever troubled about him before since his confirmation. Rolandsen would even venture to say that the priest ought to send many such letters out among his flock, to the better comfort and guidance of all.

But no one could see from Rolandsen's manner that he had been any way rejoiced or comforted of late; on the contrary, he appeared more thoughtful than ever, and seemed to be occupied with some particular thought. Shall I, or shall I not? he might be heard to murmur. And now, this morning, when his former betrothed, Jomfru van Loos, had lain in wait for him and plagued the life out of him again with that ridiculous business of the serenade, he had left her with the significant words, "I'll do it!"

Rolandsen walks into Mack's office and gives greeting. He is perfectly sober. The Macks, father and son, are standing, each at one side of the desk, writing. Old Mack offers him a chair, but Rolandsen does not sit. He says:

"I only came in to say it was me that broke in and took the money."

Father and son stare at him.

"I've come to give myself up," says Rolandsen. "It would not be right to hide it any longer; 'tis bad enough as it is."

"Leave us alone a minute," says Old Mack.

Frederik walks out.

Says Mack, "Are you in your right senses to-day?"

"I did it, I tell you," shouts Rolandsen. And Rolandsen's voice was a voice for song and strong words.

Then there was a pause. Mack blinked his eyes, and looked thoughtful. "You did it, you say?"

"Yes."

Mack thought again. That good brain of his had solved many a problem in its day; he was well used to settling a matter quickly.

"And will you hold by your words to-morrow as well?"

"Yes. From henceforth I will not conceal it. I have had a letter from the priest, and it's that has changed me."

Was Mack beginning to believe him? Or was it merely as a matter of form that he went on?

"When did you do it?" he asked.

Rolandsen mentioned the night.

"And how did you go about it?"

Rolandsen described it all in detail.

"There were some papers in the chest with the money—did you notice them?"

"Yes. There were some papers."

"One of them is missing; what have you done with it?"

"I haven't got it. A paper? No."

"My life insurance policy, it was."

"An insurance policy! Yes, now I remember. I must confess I burnt it."

"Did you? Then you ought not to have done so. It's cost me a lot of trouble to get another."

Said Rolandsen, "I was all in a flurry, and didn't think. I beg you to forgive me."

"There was another chest with several thousand *Daler* in it;

why didn't you take that?"

"I didn't find that one."

Mack had finished his calculations. Whether Rolandsen had committed the burglary or not, he would in any case make the finest culprit Mack could have wished. He would certainly make no secret of the affair, but rather declare it to every soul he met; the last boat's crew would carry the news with them home, and so it would come to the ears of the traders along the coast. Mack felt he was saved.

"I have never heard of your going about and ... your having this weakness before," he said.

Whereto Rolandsen answered, No, not among the fishermen, no. When he wanted to steal, he didn't go bird-nesting in that petty fashion; he went to the bank itself.

That was one for Mack! He only answered now with a reproachful air, "But that you could steal from *me*...."

Rolandsen said, "I worked myself up to it, to be bold enough. I was drunk at the time, I am sorry to say."

After this it seemed no longer impossible that the confession was true. Rolandsen was known to be a wild fellow who led an extravagant life and had no great income to draw upon. That keg of brandy from Rosengaard must have cost him something.

"And I've more to confess, I'm sorry to say," went on Rolandsen. "I haven't the money now, to pay it back."

Mack looked highly indifferent. "That doesn't matter in the least," he said. "The thing that troubles me is all the stupid gossip it's led to. All those unpleasant insinuations against me and my family."

"I've thought of that. And I was going to do something...."

"What do you mean?"

"Take down your placard from the Vicarage gate and put up one of my own in its place."

This was Rolandsen all over. "No," said Mack. "I won't ask you to do that. It will be hard enough for you as it is, my good man. But you might write a declaration here." And Mack nodded towards Frederik's seat.

Rolandsen set to work. Mack was thinking deeply the while. Here was all this serious business turning out for the best. It would cost him something, but the money would be well spent; his renown would now be spread far and wide.

Mack read over the declaration, and said, "Yes, that's good enough. I don't intend to make use of it, of course...."

"That's as you please," said Rolandsen.

"And I do not propose to say anything about our interview to-day. It can remain between ourselves."

"Then I shall have to tell people myself," said Rolandsen. "The priest's letter said particularly that we should confess."

Mack opened his fire-proof safe and took out a bundle of notes. Here was his chance to show what sort of man he was. And who could know that a master seiner from a stranger boat was down in the bay waiting for those very notes before he could sail?

Mack counted out four hundred *Daler*, and said, "I don't mean to insult you, but it's my way to keep to my word. I have promised a reward of four hundred *Daler*, which is now due to you."

Rolandsen walked towards the door. "I deserve your contempt," said he.

"Contempt!" said Mack. "Let me tell you...."

"Your generosity cuts me to the heart. Instead of putting me in prison, you reward me...."

But it was a mere trifle for Mack to lose a couple of hundred *Daler* over a burglary. It was only when he rewarded the thief himself with twice that amount that the thing became really magnificent. He said, "Look here, Rolandsen, you will find yourself in difficulties now; you will lose your place to begin with. The money will be no inconvenience to me, but it may be of real importance to you just now. I beg you to think over what I say."

"I couldn't do it," said Rolandsen.

Mack took the notes and thrust them into Rolandsen's pocket.

"Let it be a loan, then," said Rolandsen humbly.

And this chivalrous merchant-prince agreed, and answered, "Very well, then, as a loan." But he knew in his heart that he would never see the money again.

Rolandsen stood there looking as if weighed down by the heaviest burden in life. It was a pitiful sight.

"And now make haste and right yourself again," said Mack encouragingly. "You've made a bad slip, but it's never too late, you know."

Rolandsen thanked him with the greatest humility, and went out.

"I am a thief," he said to the factory girls as he went out, making a beginning with them without delay. And he gave them his full confession.

Then he went up to the Vicarage gate, and tore down Mack's notice, setting up his own instead. There it was in black and white, setting forth that he, Rolandsen, and no other, was the culprit. And to-morrow would be Sunday; many church-goers would pass by the spot.

X

Rolandsen seemed to be picking up again to a marked degree. After all the village had read his declaration, he kept to himself, and avoided people. This made a good impression; evidently the scapegrace had taken thought, and turned aside from his evil ways. But the fact was that Rolandsen had no time for sauntering idly about the roads now; he was restlessly at work in his room at nights. There were numbers of bottles, large and small, containing samples, that he had to pack up and send away by post east and west. Also, he was at the instrument early and late; it was essential to make the best of his time before he was dismissed.

His scandalous story had also reached the Vicarage, and everyone looked with commiseration upon Jomfru van Loos, whose former lover had turned out so badly. The priest himself called her into his study and talked to her gently for a long time.

Jomfru van Loos was certainly not now disposed to hold Rolandsen to his word; she would go and see him once more, and make an end of it.

She found him looking abject and miserable, but this did not soften her. "Nice things you've been doing," said she.

"I hoped you would come, so I could ask pardon," he answered.

"Pardon! Well, I never did! Look you here, Ove! I simply don't know what to make of you. And I'll have no more to do with you on this earth, so there. I'm not known to folk as a thief nor a rascal, but go my own honest way. And haven't I warned you faithfully from my heart, and you've only gone on as bad as ever? A man already promised and betrothed, going about as a costly jewel to other womenfolk? And then to go stealing people's money and have to stick up a confession on a gatepost in broad daylight. I'm that shamed I don't know what to do with myself. Don't say a word; I know all about you. You've nothing to say at all but only harden your heart and shout, Hurray, my boys! And it's all been true affection on my part, but you've been as a very leper towards me, and soiled my life with a disgraceful burglary. You needn't try to say a word, and only make it worse. Praise be the Lord, there's not a soul but says the same—how you've shamefully deceived me. And the priest himself says I'd better give you up and go away at once, though he'd be sorry to lose me. And it's no good you standing there trying to hide, Ove, seeing you're a sinner in the sight of God and man, and only worthy to be cast aside. And if I do call you Ove, after all that's passed, I don't mean it a bit, and you needn't think I'm going to make it up with you, because I'm not, for I won't have anything to do with you here or hereafter, and never be a friend of yours in all the world. For there's nobody could have done more for you than I've done this long time back, but you've only been overflowing with recklessness and never a thought of me, and taking advantage of me early and late. Though I'm sure it's partly my own fault, and more's the pity, by reason of being too lenient and overlooking this and that all the time."

There stood Rolandsen, a wretched creature, with never a word to say for himself. He had never heard Marie van Loos so incoherent as to-day; it showed how his dire misdeed had shaken her. When she stopped speaking, she seemed thoroughly exhausted.

"I'll turn over a new leaf," he said.

"You? A new leaf?" Jomfru van Loos laughed bitterly. "What's done is done, and will be for all your turning. And seeing I'm come of decent folk myself, I'll not have you smirching my good name. When I say a thing, I mean it. And I tell you now, I'm going away by the post-packet the day after to-morrow; but I'm not going to have you coming down to the quay saying good-bye, and the priest he says the same. I'll say good-bye to you to-day and once and for all. And thanks for the happy hours we've had together—the rest I'll try to forget."

She swung round determinedly and walked away. Then she said, "But you can be up in the woods just above, if you like, and wave good-bye from there—not that I care if you do or don't."

"You might shake hands," he said.

"No, I won't. You know only too well what your right hand doeth."

Rolandsen stood bowed and downcast. "But aren't we to write?" he said. "Only just a word or so?"

"I won't write. Never on earth. You've said often enough it was all over between us, and made a joke of it; but now I'm good enough, it seems. But I know better! It's good-bye for ever, and I wish you joy. I'm going to Bergen, to stay with father, and you know the address if you write. But I won't ask you to."

Rolandsen went up the steps to his room with a very clear sensation of being betrothed no longer. "Curious thing," he thought to himself, "I was standing down there outside a moment ago."

It was a busy day; he had to pack up the last of his samples ready to go by the post-packet the day after to-morrow; then he had to collect his own belongings and prepare for the moving. The all-powerful Inspector of the Telegraphs was on the way.

Of course he would be summarily dismissed. There was nothing to be said against him in respect of his duties, and Trader Mack, a man of great influence, would doubtless do nothing to harm him, but for all that, justice must be done.

There was grass in the meadows now, and the woods were in leaf; the nights were mild and calm. The bay was deserted, all the fishing-boats were gone, and Mack's own vessels had sailed away to the southward with their cargoes of herring. It was summer.

The fine days gave good attendance at the church on Sundays; crowds of people came by land and water, and among them a few skippers from Bergen and Haugesund, who had their craft out along the coast, drying split fish on the rocks. They came again year after year, and grew old in the place. They turned up at church in full dress, with bright calico shirts and chains of hair down over their chests; some of them even wore gold earrings, and brightened up the assembly. But the dry weather brought news of a regrettable forest fire farther up the fjords; summer weather was not all for the good.

Enok had entered upon his office, and was lay-helper now in earnestness and all humility, with a kerchief over his ears. The youth of the village found great amusement in the sight, but their elders were inclined to be scandalised at having the choir disgraced by monkey figures of the sort, and sent in a complaint to the priest about it. Could not Enok manage with stuffing wadding in his ears? But Enok explained to the priest that he could not put away the kerchief by reason of the aches and pains that raged tumultuously within. Then it was that ex-Lay-helper Levion set up a malicious laughter at his supplanter Enok, and opined that it was hot enough for most these days without tying kerchiefs round their ears.

Levion, unworthy soul, had, since his downfall, never ceased from persecuting Enok with jealousy and ill-will. Never a night he was out spearing flounder but he must choose his place off Enok's shore and beach, and spear such flounder as had been nearest Enok's hand. And if he chanced to need a thole-pin or a bit of wood for a baling scoop, it was always in Enok's fir-copse close to the water that he sought it. He kept a constant eye on Enok himself.

It was soon noised abroad that Jomfru van Loos had broken off her engagement, and in the depth of that disgrace was leaving the Vicarage at once. Trader Mack felt that Rolandsen, poor fellow, was having trouble enough over the affair, and endeavoured now himself to heal the breach. He took down Rolandsen's announcement with his own hands from the gatepost, and declared that it was by no wish of his it had been set there at all. Then he went down to the Vicarage. Mack could afford to be tolerant now; he had already marked what a profound impression his generous behaviour in the burglary affair had produced. People greeted him now as respectfully as ever,—even, it seemed, with greater esteem than before. Surely there was but one Mack on all the coast!

But his visit to the Vicarage proved of no avail. Jomfru van Loos was moved even to tears at the thought of Mack's coming in person, but no one on earth should persuade her now to make it up with Rolandsen, never! Mack gathered that it was the priest who had brought her to such a pitch of determination.

When Jomfru van Loos went down to the boat, her master and mistress saw her off. Both wished her a pleasant journey, and watched her get into the boat.

"Oh, Heaven," said Jomfru van Loos, "I know he's up there in the woods this minute and bitterly repenting." And she took out her handkerchief.

The boat pushed off and glided away under long strokes.

"There he is!" cried Jomfru van Loos, half rising. She looked for a moment as if about to wade ashore. Then she fell to waving with all her might up towards the woods. And the boat disappeared round the point.

Rolandsen went home through the woods as he had taken to doing of late; but coming opposite the Vicarage fence, he moved down on to the road and followed it. Well, now all his samples were sent off, he had nothing to do but await the result. It would not take long. And Rolandsen snapped his fingers from sheer lightness of heart as he walked.

A little farther on sat Olga, the parish clerk's daughter, on a stone by the roadside. What was she doing there? Rolandsen thought to himself: She must be coming from the store, and waiting for somebody here. A little later came Elise Mack. Oho! were they inseparables now? She too sat down, and seemed to be waiting. Now was the time to delight the ladies by appearing crushed and humbled, a very worm, thought Rolandsen to himself. He turned off hurriedly into the wood. But the dried twigs crackled underfoot; they could hear him. It would be a fruitless attempt, and he gave it up. Might go down the road again, he thought; no need to delight them overmuch. And he walked down along the road.

But it was not so easy after all to face Elise Mack. His heart began to beat heavily, a sudden warmth flowed through him, and he stopped. He had gained nothing that last time, and since then a great misdeed had been added against him. He drew off backward into the wood again. If only he were past this clearing, the dry twigs would come to an end and the heather begin. He took it in a few long strides, and was saved. Suddenly he stopped; what the devil was he hopping about like this for? He, Ove Rolandsen! He turned, and strode defiantly back across the clearing, tramping over dry twigs as loudly as

75

he pleased.

Coming down on to the road again, he saw the ladies still seated in the same place. They were talking, and Elise was digging at the ground with the point of her parasol. Rolandsen halted again. Your dare-devil sort are ever the most cautious. "But I'm a thief," he said to himself. "How can I have the face to show myself? If I give a greeting, it will be forcing them to recognise me." And once more he drew back among the trees. What a fool he was, to go about with such feelings—as if he had not other things to think about! A couple of months hence he would be rich, a man of wealth and position. In love? The devil take all such fancies. And he turned his steps towards home.

Were they sitting there still, he wondered. He turned and stole a glance. Frederik had joined them, and here they were all three coming towards him. He hurried back, with his heart in his mouth. If only they had not seen him! They stopped, and he heard Frederik Mack say, "Sh! There's someone in the wood."—"Oh, it's nothing," answered Elise.

Like as not she said so because she had seen him, thought Rolandsen. And the thought made him cold and bitter all at once. No, of course, he was nothing—nothing as yet. But wait, only two months.... And anyhow, what was she herself? A Virgin Mary cold as iron, daughter of the Lutheran celebrity Mack of Rosengaard. *Bliv i Freden!*

There was a weathercock on the roof of the telegraph station, perched on an iron rod. Rolandsen came home, climbed up to the roof, and bent that iron rod with his own hands, till the cock leaned backward, as if in the act of crowing. Let it stand so; it was only right the cock should crow.

XI

A nd now sets in a time of easy days for all, no fishing beyond the little for home needs; fishing on warm, sunny nights—a pleasant task, a pastime. Corn and potatoes growing, and meadows waving; herring stored in every shed, and cows and goats milking full pails, and rolling in fat themselves.

Mack and his daughter Elise have gone back home again; Frederik reigns alone over the factory and the store. And Frederik's rule is none of the best; he is full of his own thoughts of the sea, and hates this life on shore. Captain Henriksen of the coasting steamer has half promised to get him a berth as mate on board his vessel, but it never seems to come to anything. Then comes the question whether old Mack will buy a steamer himself for his son to run. He talks of it, and seems willing enough, but Frederik guesses it is more than he can do. Frederik knows the position pretty well. He is strangely little of a seaman by nature, a cautious and reliable youth, doing just as much of this thing and that as is needed in his daily life. He takes after his mother, and is not altogether the true Mack type. But that is well for one who would get on in the world and succeed; never do too much, but rather a little too little of everything, so it could be reckoned as just enough. Look at Rolandsen, for instance, that extravagant madcap with his wild fancies. A common thief among his fellows, that was what he had come to, and lost his position into the bargain. And there he was, going about with a burdened conscience, wearing his clothes down thinner and thinner, and never so much as a room of his own to live in, saving a bit of a bedroom at Børre the organ-blower's, and that was humble enough. That was the end of Ove Rolandsen. Børre might be an excellent man in his way, but he was the poorest in the place, and had least herring in his store. And seeing his daughter Pernille was a poor, weakly creature, the organ-blower's house was never reckoned for much. It was not the place a man of any decent position could choose to live in.

It was said that Rolandsen might have avoided dismissal if only he had behaved with proper contrition towards the visiting Inspector. But Rolandsen had simply taken it for granted that he was to be dismissed, and had given the Inspector no opportunity of pardoning him. And old Mack, the mediator, was not there.

But the priest was not altogether displeased with Rolandsen. "I've heard he drinks less than he used to," he said. "And I should not regard him as altogether lost. He himself admits that it was a letter from me that led him to confess about the burglary. It is encouraging to see one's work bear fruit now and again."

Midsummer's eve came round, and fires were lit on high places, young men and girls from the fisher-huts gathered about the fires, fiddles and concertinas were heard about the village. The best way was to make only the least little fire, but heaps of smoke; damp moss and juniper twigs were flung on the fires to make the smoke properly thick and scented.

Rolandsen was still unabashed enough to take part in the popular festivity; he sat on a big rock thrumming at his guitar, and singing till the valley echoed again. When he came down and joined those about the fire, he was seen to be as drunk as an owl, and overflowing with magnificent speech. The same as ever; an incorrigible.

But then came Olga walking down the road. She had never a thought of stopping here; she was but walking that way and would have passed by. Oh, she might well have gone another way; but Olga was young, and the music of the concertina drew her; her nostrils quivered, a fountain of happiness was in her—she was in love. She had been to the store earlier in the day, and Frederik Mack had said words enough for her to understand, for all he spoke with caution. And now, perhaps he too might be out for a walk this evening!

Fruen came down from the Vicarage; the two walked on together, talking of no other than Frederik Mack. He was the lord of the village, and even Fruen's heart had bowed to him in secret; he was so nice and careful, and kept to earth at every step. Fruen noticed at last that Olga was overcome with shyness about something, and asked, "But, child, what makes you so quiet? Surely you haven't fallen in love with this young Mack?"

"Yes," whispered Olga, bursting into tears.

Fruen stopped, "Olga, Olga! And does he care for you?"

"I think he does."

And at that Fruen's eyes grew quiet and stupid-looking again, and gazed emptily into air. "Well, well," she said, with a smile. "Heaven bless you, child; it will come all right, you see." And she was kinder than ever to Olga after that.

When they reached the Vicarage, the priest was walking up and down in great excitement. "The woods are on fire," he cried. "I could see it from the window." And he got a supply of axes and picks and men, and manned his boat down at the waterside. It was Enok's copse that was burning.

But ahead of the priest and his party went ex-Lay-helper Levion. Levion had been out seeing to his lines; he had set them as usual just off Enok's ground, and caught a decent batch. Then on the way back he saw a tiny flame break out in the wood, and grow bigger and bigger. Levion nodded a little to himself, as if he understood what a little flame like that might mean. And then, seeing folk moving busily about round the priest's boathouse, he understands they have come down to help; he heads his boat round and puts in at once, to be first on the spot. It was beautiful to see him laying aside all enmity at once and hurrying to his rival's aid.

Levion puts in to shore and moves up at once to the wood; he can hear the roar of the fire already. He takes his time, looking round carefully at every step; presently he spies Enok coming along in the greatest haste. Levion is seized with great excitement; he slips behind an overhanging rock and peers out from cover. Enok comes nearer, moving with a purpose, looking neither right nor left, but coming straight on. Had he discovered his enemy, and was coming to seek him? When he was quite close up, Levion gave a hail. Enok started, and came to a halt. And in his confusion he smiled, and said:

"Here's a fire, worse luck. There's trouble abroad."

The other took courage, and answered, "'Twill be the finger of God, no doubt."

Enok frowned. "What are you standing about here for?" he asked.

All Levion's hatred flares up now, and he says, "Ho-ho! 'Twill be over-hot for kerchiefs round the ears now."

"Get away with you!" says Enok. "Like as not it was you that started the fire."

But Levion was blind and deaf. Enok seemed to be making towards just that corner of the rock where Levion stood.

"Keep off!" cries Levion. "I've torn off one of your ears already—do you want me to take the other?"

"Get away with you, d'you hear?" says Enok, coming closer.

Levion was choking and swallowing with anger. He cried

out loud, "Remember that day in the fjord, when I caught you pulling up my lines? I twisted one ear off then...."

And that was why Enok went about with a kerchief round his head; he had but one ear. And both he and Levion had very good reasons for keeping quiet about the matter.

"You're no better than a murderer, to speak of," said Enok.

The priest's boat was heard rushing in to land, and from the other side came the roar of the fire, ever nearer. Enok writhed, and tried again to make Levion retreat; he drew his knife—that excellent knife for cutting things.

Levion rolled his eyes and screamed out, "As sure as you dare come waving knives at me, there's folk at hand already, and here they come!"

Enok put up his knife again. "What d'you want standing there anyway?" he said. "Get away with you!"

"What are you doing here yourself, anyway?"

"What's that to you? I've an errand here; some things I've hidden here. And there's the fire all close up."

But Levion stayed defiantly, and would not move an inch. Here was the priest coming up, and he, no doubt, could hear the two in dispute—but what did Levion care for him now?

The boat lay to, and those on board rushed up with axe and pick. The priest gave a brief greeting and a hasty word. "These midsummer bonfires are dangerous, Enok; the sparks fly about all over the place. Where had we better begin?"

Enok was at a loss for the moment; the priest had put him out, and drew him away now, so that he could not deal with Levion further.

"Which way's the wind?" asked the priest. "Come and show us where to start digging."

But Enok was desperately ill at ease; he looked round anxiously for Levion, and answered at random.

"Do not give way so," said the priest. "Pull yourself together, and be a man. We must get the fire under." And he took Enok by the arm.

Some of the men had already moved forward towards the fire, and were digging across its path. Levion was still in his old place, breathing hard; he kicked at a flat stone that lay in under the rock. "He won't have hidden anything here," thought Levion to himself. "It was just a lie." But he looked down again, and, kicking away some of the earth, he came upon a kerchief. One of Enok's kerchiefs it was—a quondam bandage for the earache. Levion picked it up; there was something wrapped in it. He unfastened it, and there was money—paper money— notes, and many of them. Furthermore, there was a document, a big white sheet. Levion was full of curiosity. He thought at once, "Stolen money!" And he unfolded the document and began to spell it through.

Then it was that Enok caught sight of him, and gave a hoarse cry; breaking away from the priest, he rushed back towards Levion, knife in hand.

"Enok, Enok!" cried the priest, making after him.

"Here is the thief!" cried Levion, as they came up.

The priest fancied Enok must have gone suddenly demented at sight of the fire. "Put up your knife!" he called out.

Levion went on, "Here's the burglar that stole Mack's money."

"What's that you say?" asked the priest uncomprehendingly.

Enok makes a dash at his opponent, and tries to snatch the packet away.

"Get out! I'm going to hand it over to the priest," cries Levion. "And he can see for himself the sort of helper he's got now."

Enok staggered to a tree; his face was grey. The priest looks blankly at the paper, the kerchief, and the notes; he can make nothing of it all.

"I found it there," says Levion, shaking all over. "He'd hidden it under a stone. There's Mack's name on the paper, you can see."

The priest examined it, growing more and more astounded as he read. "This must be the insurance policy Mack said he had lost, surely?"

"And the money he lost as well," said Levion.

Enok pulled himself together. "Then you must have put it there," he said.

The roar of the forest fire came nearer, the air was growing hotter and hotter about them, but the three men stood still.

"I know nothing about it," said Enok again. "It's just a trick of Levion's, to do me harm."

Said Levion, "Here's two hundred *Daler*. Have I ever had two hundred *Daler* in my life? And isn't this your kerchief? Isn't it one you've worn over your ears?"

"Yes, isn't that so?" seconded the priest.

Enok was silent.

The priest was counting over the notes. "There are not two hundred *Daler* here," he said.

"He's spent some of it, of course," said Levion.

But Enok stood breathing heavily. "I know nothing about it," he said. "But as for you, Levion, you see if I don't remember you for this!"

The priest was utterly at a loss. If Enok were the thief, then Rolandsen had only been making a jest of the letter he had sent him. And what for?

The heat was growing unbearable; the three men moved down towards the water, the fire at their heels. They were forced to get into the boat, and then to push off away from land altogether.

"Anyhow, this is Mack's policy," said the priest. "We must

report what has happened. Row back home, Levion."

Enok was annihilated, and sat staring gloomily before him. "Ay, let's go and report it," he said. "That's all I want."

The priest gave him a troubled look. "Do you, I wonder?" he said. And he closed his eyes in horror at the whole affair.

Enok, in his covetousness, had been too simple. He had carefully preserved the insurance paper that he could make nothing of. It was an imposing-looking document, with stamps on, and a great sum of money written there; who could say but he might be able to go away some day and sell it? It was surely too valuable to throw away.

The priest turned and looked back at the fire. Men were at work in the woods, trees were falling, and a broad trench was spreading darkly across. More helpers had come up to join in the work.

"The fire'll stop of itself," said Levion.

"Do you think so?"

"Soon as it gets to the birches it'll stop."

And the boat with the three men on board rowed in to the Lensmand's.

XII

When the priest came back that evening he had been weeping. Evil and wrong-doing seemed to flourish all about him. He was wounded and humbled with sorrow; now his wife could not even have the shoes she needed so badly. Enok's rich offering would have to be returned to the giver, as being stolen goods. And that would leave the priest blank and bare.

He went up to his wife at once. But even before he had passed the door of her room, new trouble and despair came to meet him. His wife was sewing. Garments were strewn about the floor, a fork and a dishcloth from the kitchen lay on the bed, together with newspapers and some crochet-work. One of her slippers was on the table. On her chest of drawers lay a branch of birch in leaf and a big grey pebblestone.

He set about, from force of habit, putting things in order.

"You've no need to trouble," said she. "I was going to put that slipper away myself as soon as I'd done my sewing."

"But how can you sit and work with the place in such a mess?"

At this she was offended, and made no answer.

"What do you want that stone for?" he asked.

"It's not for anything particular. I just found it on the beach, and it was so pretty."

He swept up a little heap of faded grass that lay beside the mirror, and put it in a newspaper.

"I don't know if you want this for anything?" he asked, checking himself.

"No, it's no good now. It's sorrel; I was going to use it for a salad."

"It's been lying here over a week," he said. "And it's made a stain here on the polish."

"There, that shows you. Polished furniture's such a nuisance; I can't see any sense in it myself."

At that he burst out into an angry laugh. His wife dropped her work and stood up.

He could never leave her in peace, but was always worrying the life out of her with his lack of sense. And so they drifted once more into one of the foolish, fruitless quarrels that had been repeated at intervals through the past four years. The priest had come up in all humility to beg his wife's indulgence because he could not get her the new shoes at once, but he found it now more and more impossible to carry out his purpose; bitterness overpowered him. Things were all wrong every way at the Vicarage since Jomfru van Loos had left them and his wife had taken over the housekeeping herself.

"And while I think of it, I wish you would use a little sense and thought over things in the kitchen," he said.

"Sense and thought? And don't I, then? Do you mean to say things are worse now than before?"

"I found the dust-bin full of good food yesterday."

"If only you wouldn't go interfering with everything...."

"I found a dish of cream from the dinner the other day."

"Well, the maids had been at it, and I didn't care to use it after them."

"I found a lot of rice as well."

"It was the milk had turned, and spoiled it. I couldn't help that, could I?"

"One day I found a boiled egg, with the shell off, in the dust-bin."

His wife was silent. Though, indeed, she could have found

something to say to that as well.

"We're not exactly rich enough to waste things," said the priest. "And you know yourself we have to pay for the eggs. One day the cat was eating an omelette."

"Only a bit that was left from dinner. But you're all unreasonable, and that's the truth; you ought to see a doctor for that temper of yours."

"I've seen you stand holding the cat and pushing a bowl of milk under its nose. And you let the maids see it too. They laugh at you behind your back."

"They *don't*. It's only you that are always nasty and ill-tempered."

The end of it was that the priest went back to his study, and his wife was left in peace.

At breakfast next morning no one could see from her looks that she had been suffering and wretched. All her trouble seemed charmed away, and not a memory of their quarrel left. Her easy, changeable nature stood her in good stead, and helped to make her life endurable. The priest was touched once more. After all, he might as well have held his peace about these household matters; the new housekeeper would be coming soon, and should be on her way already.

"I'm sorry you'll hardly be able to get those shoes just yet," he said.

"No, no," was all she said.

"Enok's offering will have to be returned; the money was stolen."

"What's that you say?"

"Yes, only fancy—it was he who stole all that money from Mack. He confessed before the *Lensmand* yesterday." And the priest told her the whole story.

"Then it wasn't Rolandsen after all..." said Fruen.

"Oh, Rolandsen—he's always in mischief some way or other. An incorrigible fellow. But, anyhow, I'm afraid your shoes will have to wait again."

"Oh, but it doesn't matter about the shoes."

That was her way, always kind and unselfish to the last—a mere child. And her husband had never heard her complain about their poverty.

"If only you could wear mine," he said, softening.

But at that she laughed heartily. "Yes, and you wear mine instead, ha-ha-ha!" And here she dropped his plate on the floor and smashed it; dropped the cold cutlet as well. "Wait a minute; I'll fetch another plate," she said, and hurried out.

Never a word about the damage, thought the priest; never so much as entered her head. And plates cost money.

"But you're surely not going to eat that cutlet?" said his wife when she came in.

"Why, what else should we do with it?"

"Give it to the cat, of course."

"I'm afraid I can't afford that sort of thing, if you can," said he, turning gloomy again. And this might have led to a first-rate quarrel again, if she had not been wise enough to pass it over in silence. As it was, both felt suddenly out of spirits....

Next day another remarkable happening was noised abroad: Rolandsen had disappeared. On hearing the news of the find in the wood, and Enok's confession, he had exclaimed, "The devil! It's come too early—by a month, at least." Børre the organ-blower had heard it. Then, later in the evening, Rolandsen was nowhere to be found, within doors or without. But Børre's little boat, that was drawn up at the Vicarage landing-place, had disappeared, together with oars and fishing-gear and all that was in it.

Word was sent to Rosengaard at once about the discovery

of the true thief, but, strangely enough, Mack seemed in no hurry to come back and take the matter up anew. Doubtless he had his reasons. Rolandsen had cheated him into paying out a reward, and he would now have to pay the same sum over again, which was by no means convenient at the moment. A true Mack, he would never think of acting less open-handedly now than before,—it was a point of honour with him,—but just at the moment he was pressed for money. Mack's numerous and various undertakings called for considerable disbursements, and there had been no great influx of ready cash for some time past. There was his big consignment of herring still in the hands of the agents at Bergen; prices were low, and Mack was holding. He waited impatiently for the dog-days; after that, the fishing would be definitely at an end, and prices would go up. Also, the Russians were at war, and agriculture in that widespread land would be neglected; the population would need fish to help them out.

Weeks passed, and Mack failed to appear at the factory at all. There was that bakery, too, that he had promised the people at the Vicarage—and what was he to say when Fruen asked him? The foundations were laid, and the ground had been levelled, but no building was being done. Once more folk began to whisper about Mack; how, like as not, he would find it awkward to get on with that bakery place. So strong was this feeling of doubt, that the baker at the *Lensmand's* took to drink again. He felt himself secure; a bakery could not be run up in a week; there was time at any rate for a good solid bout. The priest heard of his backsliding, and appealed to him in person, but with little effect; the man felt safe at least for the time being.

And in truth, the priest, who was ever a worker, had much on his hands just now; he spared no effort, but for all that he seemed always behindhand. And now he had lost one of his helpers, the most zealous of them all—Enok to wit. Only a couple of days after that disaster, Levion had come up once more, and showed himself extremely willing to be reinstated.

"Priest can see now, surely, there's none could be better for the place than me."

"H'm! You are suspected of having started that fire yourself."

"'Tis an everlasting thief and scoundrel said that lie!" exclaimed Levion.

"Good! But anyhow, you're not going to be helper again."

"Who's it to be this time, then?"

"No one. I shall manage without."

That sort of man was the priest; strong and stiff and just in his dealings with all. And he had reason now to mortify himself without pity. The constant discomfort at home and the many difficulties of his office were striving to demoralise him and tempt him to his fall; reprehensible thoughts came into his head at times. Why, for instance, should he not make peace with Levion, who could be useful to him in many little matters by way of return? Furthermore, Mack of Rosengaard had offered his help in any deserving case of actual need. Well and good! He, the priest himself, was in greater need than any of his flock. Why not apply to Mack for help on behalf of a family in distress, and keep the help so given for himself? Then he could get that pair of shoes for his wife. He himself needed one or two little things as well—a few books, a little philosophy; he felt himself withering up in the round of daily toil; his development was checked. Rolandsen, that glib-tongued rogue, had declared it was human beings had made God what He was, and the priest had marked the effect of that upon his own wife. He needed books from which to arm himself for the abolishment of Rolandsen as soon as opportunity arose.

Mack came at last—came, as usual, in splendour and state;

his daughter Elise was with him. He called at the Vicarage at once, as a matter of courtesy; moreover, he did not in any way desire to hide away from his promise. Fruen asked about the bakery. Mack regretted that he had been unable to get the work done sooner, but there were very good reasons. It was a flat impossibility to get the building done this year; the foundations must have time to settle first. Fruen gave a little cry of disappointment, but her husband was relieved.

"That's what the experts tell me," said Mack. "And what can I do? If we were to build and finish now, then next spring's thaw might shift the whole foundation several inches. And what would happen to the building above?"

"Yes, of course," agreed the priest.

But it must not be thought that Mack was in any way discouraged; far from it. The dog-days were past, the herring fishery was at an end, and the agent in Bergen had wired that prices were going up by leaps and bounds. Mack could not help telling them the news at the Vicarage. And in return the priest was able to inform him where Rolandsen was hiding, on an island among the outer reefs, far to the west, like a wild savage. A man and woman had come up to the Vicarage and brought the news.

Mack sent off a boat at once in search.

XIII

The fact of the matter was, that Enok's confession had taken Rolandsen all unawares. He was free now, but, on the other hand, he had not the four hundred *Daler* to pay Mack. And so it came about that he took the boat, with Børre's gear and tackle, and rowed away in the silent night. He made for the outer islands, and that was a six-mile journey, part of it over open sea. He rowed all night, and looked about in the morning till he found a suitable island. Here he landed; wild birds of all sorts flew up about him.

Rolandsen was hungry; his first thought was to gather a score of gull's eggs and make a meal. But he found the eggs all addled. Then he rowed out fishing, and had more luck. And now he lived on fish from day to day, and sang and wore the time away, and was lord of that island. When it rained, he had a first-rate shelter under an overhanging rock. He slept on a grassy patch at night, and the sun never set.

Two weeks, three weeks, passed. Rolandsen grew desperately thin from his wretched mode of life, but his eyes grew harder and harder from sheer determination, and he would not give in. His only fear was that someone might come and disturb him. A few nights back there had come a boat, a man and a woman in it—a pair out gathering down. They would have landed on the island, but Rolandsen was by no means that way inclined. He had sighted them afar off, and had time to work himself up into a fury, so that when they arrived, he made such threatening play with Børre's tiny anchor that the couple rowed away in fright. Then Rolandsen laughed to himself, and a most uncomely fiend he was to look at, with his hollow cheeks.

One morning the birds made more noise than usual, and Rolandsen awoke, though it was still so early as to be almost night. He sees a boat making in, already close at hand. It was always a trouble with Rolandsen that he was so slow to anger. Here was this boat coming in, and its coming highly inconvenient to him just then, but by the time he had worked up an adequate rage, the men had landed. If only they had given him time, he might have done something to stop them; might have pelted them to rags with stones from the beach.

They were two of Mack's folk from the factory, father and son. They stepped ashore, and "*Goddag!*" said the older one.

"I'm not the least little pleased to see you, and I'll do you a hurt," said Rolandsen.

"Ho, and how'll you do that?" said the man, with a look at his son, but not very bold for all that.

"Throttle you dead, for instance. What do you say to that little plan?"

"'Twas Mack himself that sent us to find you here."

"Of course it was Mack himself. I know well enough what he wants."

Then the younger man put in a word, and this was that Børre the organ-blower wanted his boat and gear.

Rolandsen shouted bitterly at that. "Børre! Is the fellow mad? And what about me then? Here am I living on a desert island; I must have a boat to get to folk, and gear to fish with, if I'm not to starve. Tell him that from me!"

"And then there was a word from the new man at the station, how there's telegrams waiting for you there. Important."

Rolandsen jumped. Already! He asked a question or so, which they answered, and thereafter he made no further objection, but went back with them. The younger man rowed

Børre's boat, and Rolandsen sat in the other.

There was a provision-box in the forepart of the boat, that waked in his mind impertinent hopes of food. He was on the point of asking if they had brought anything to eat with them, but restrained himself, out of sheer lordliness and pride, and tried to talk it off.

"How did Mack know I was here?"

"'Twas the news came. A man and a woman saw you here one night; you frightened them a deal."

"Well, what did they want here anyway? And I've hit on a new fishing-ground there by the island. And now I'm leaving it."

"How long'd you thought to be staying there?"

"'Tis no business of yours," said Rolandsen sharply. His eyes were fixed on that provision-box, but he showed himself as ready to burst, out of sheer pride, and said, "It's more than commonly ugly, that box there. Shouldn't think anyone'd care to keep food in a thing like that. What d'you use it for?"

"If only I'd all the butter and cheese and pork and butcher's meat's been in that box, I'd not go hungry for years to come," answered the man.

Rolandsen cleared his throat, and spat over the side.

"When did those telegrams come?" he asked.

"Eh, that'll be some time back."

Half-way across, the two boats closed in and lay alongside; father and son brought out their meal from the box, and Rolandsen looked all other ways. Said the old man, "We've a bite of food here, if as you're not too proud." And they passed the whole box across.

But Rolandsen waved it away, and answered:

"I'm fed, no more than half an hour since. As much as I could eat. That cake of bread there looks uncommonly nicely done, though. No, no, thanks; I was only looking at it ... smells nice, too...."

And Rolandsen chattered away, looking to every other side.

"We're never short of plenty these parts, and that's the truth," he went on. "I'll wager now there's not a hut nor shed but's got its leg of meat hung up. But there's no need to be always eating so much; 'tis a beastly fashion."

He writhed uncomfortably on his seat, and went on:

"How long I was going to stay there, d'you say? Why, I'd have stayed till the autumn, to see the shooting stars. I've a great fancy for such things; it tickles me to see whole planets go to pieces."

"There you're talking more than I know of."

"Planets, man—stars. Butting into one another all across the sky. 'Tis a wild and wicked sight."

But the men went on eating, and at last Rolandsen could contain himself no longer. "What pigs you are to eat, you two! Stuffing all that into you at once—I never saw...."

"We've done," said the old man quietly enough.

The boats pushed apart, and the two men bent to their oars. Rolandsen lay back and tried to sleep.

It was afternoon when they got in, and Rolandsen went up to the station at once for his telegrams. There were encouraging messages about his invention; a high bid for the patent rights from Hamburg, and a still higher one from another firm through the bureau. And Rolandsen, in his incomprehensible fashion, must needs run off to the woods and stay there alone for quite a while before he thought of getting a bite to eat. The excess of feeling made him a boy again; he was as a child, with folded hands.

XIV

He went to Mack's office, and went thither as a man come to his own, ay, as a lion. There would be strange feelings in the Mack family at seeing him again. Elise, maybe, would congratulate him, and kindliness from her would be a joy.

But he was disappointed. He came upon Elise outside the factory, talking to her brother; she paid so little heed to him that his greeting all but passed unanswered. And the pair went on talking as before. Rolandsen would not disturb them by asking for old Mack, but went up to the office and knocked at the door. It was locked. He went down again and said, "Your father sent for me; where shall I find him?"

The two were in no hurry to answer, but finished what they had to say. Then said Frederik, "Father's up at the watergate."

"Might have said that when I came up first," thought Rolandsen. Oh, they were all indifferent to him now; they had let him go up to the office without a word.

"Couldn't you send word to him?" asked Rolandsen.

Said Frederik slowly, "When father's up at the watergate, he's there because he's business there."

Rolandsen looked at the two with eyes of wonder.

"Better come again later on," said Frederik.

"If I come a second time, it'll be to say I shan't come a third."

Frederik shrugged his shoulders.

"There's father," said Elise.

Old Mack came walking towards them. He frowned, spoke sharply, and walked on ahead of Rolandsen to the office. All ungraciousness. Then he said:

"Last time, I asked you to sit down. This time, I don't."

"No, no," said Rolandsen. But he was puzzled at the other's angry manner.

But Mack found no pleasure in being harsh. He had power over this man, who had done him a wrong, and he preferred to show himself too proud to use it. He said, "You know, of course, what has happened here?"

Said Rolandsen, "I have been away. Things may have happened that you know of, but not I."

"I'll tell you how it is, then," said Mack. And Mack was now as a minor God, with the fate of a human creature in his hand. "You burnt up that insurance policy, I think you said?"

"Well, not exactly," said Rolandsen. "To tell the truth...."

"Here it is," said Mack, and brought out the document. "The money has been found, too. The whole lot was found wrapped up in a kerchief that did *not* belong to you."

Rolandsen made no protest.

"It belonged to Enok," Mack went on.

Rolandsen could not help smiling at the other's solemn manner, and said jestingly, "Ah, now I shouldn't be surprised if it was Enok was the thief."

Mack found this tone by no means to his taste; it was lacking in respect. "You've made a fool of me," he said, "and cheated me out of four hundred *Daler*."

Rolandsen, with his precious telegrams in his pocket, still found it hard to be serious. "Let's talk it over a little," said he.

Then said Mack sharply, "Last time, I forgave you. This time, I don't."

"I can pay you back the money."

Mack turned on him angrily. "The money's no more to me now than it was then. But you're a cheat; do you realise that?"

"If you'll allow me, I'll explain."

"No."

"Well, now, that's all unreasonable," said Rolandsen, still smiling. "What do you want with me at all, then?"

"I'm going to have you locked up," said Mack.

Frederik came in, and went to his place at the desk. He had heard the last words, and saw his father now, for once, in a state of excitement.

Rolandsen thrust his hand into his pocket, where the telegrams lay, and said, "Won't you accept the money, then?"

"No," said Mack. "You can hand it over to the authorities."

Rolandsen stood there still. Nothing of a lion now; properly speaking, he had made a big mistake, and might be put in prison. Well and good! And when Mack looked at him inquiringly, as if to ask what he might be standing there for, he answered, "I'm waiting to be locked up."

"Here?" Mack looked at him in astonishment. "No, you can go along home and get ready."

"Thanks. I've some telegrams to send off."

Mack turned gentler all at once. After all, he was not a savage. "I'll give you to-day and to-morrow to get ready," he said.

Rolandsen bowed, and went out.

Elise was still standing outside; he passed by her this time without a sign. What was lost was lost; there was no helping it now.

But Elise called to him softly, and he stopped, stood gazing at her, shaken and confused in his surprise.

"I—I was only going to say ... it's nothing serious, is it?"

Rolandsen could make nothing of this; could not understand why she had suddenly chosen to speak to him at all. "I've got leave to go home," he said. "To send off some telegrams."

She came up close to him, her breast heaving; she looked

round, as if in fear of something. Then she said:

"Father was angry, I suppose. But it'll soon pass off, I'm sure."

Rolandsen was offended; had he himself no right in the case? "Your father can do as he pleases," he said.

Ho, so that was his tone! But Elise breathed heavily as before, and said, "Why do you look at me like that? Don't you know me again?"

Grace and kindliness without end. Rolandsen answered, "As to knowing again or not, that's as folk themselves will have it."

Pause. Then said Elise at last, "But surely you can see, after what you've done ... still, it's worst for yourself."

"Good! Let it be worst for myself then. I'm not going to be called to account by all and sundry—I won't stand it. Your father can have me locked up if he likes."

She turned without a word and left him....

***

Rolandsen waited for two days—waited for three, but there came none to the organ-blower's house to arrest him. He was in dire excitement. He had written out his telegrams, ready to send off the moment he was arrested; he would accept the highest bid for his invention, and sell the patent. Meantime, he was not idle; he kept the foreign firms busy with negotiations about this and that, such as purchase of the falls above Mack's factory, and guarantees of transport facilities. All these matters were left in his hands for the present.

But Mack was not inclined to persecute a fellow-creature just now; on the contrary, his business was going excellently, and as long as things went well, it pleased him far more to be generous beyond need. A new telegram from the agent in Bergen had informed him that the fish was sold to Russia; if Mack had need of money, money was at his disposal. Altogether, Mack was getting on swimmingly again.

When over a week had passed without any change, Rolandsen went down to Mack's office again. He was worn out with anxiety and uncertainty; he felt he must have a decision.

"I've been waiting a week, and you haven't had me arrested yet," he said.

"Young man," said Mack indulgently, "I have been thinking over your affair...."

"Old man," said Rolandsen violently, "you'll please to settle it now! You think you can go on for ever and ever and be mightily gracious as long as you please, but I'll soon put a stop to that. I'll give myself up to the police."

"Really, this tone," said Mack, "it's not what I should have expected from you, considering...."

"I'll show you what you can expect from me," cried Rolandsen, with unnecessary arrogance. And he flung down his telegrams on the desk. Rolandsen's big nose looked even more aggressive than usual, since he had got thinner in the face.

Mack glanced through the messages. "So you've turned inventor?" he said carelessly. But as he read on, he screwed up his eyes intently. "Fish-glue," said he at last. And then he went through the telegrams once more.

"This looks very promising," he said, looking up. "Am I to understand you've been offered all this money for a fish-glue process of your own?"

"Yes."

"Then I congratulate you. But surely you must feel it beneath your dignity now to behave rudely towards an old man."

"You're right there, of course; yes. But I'm all worn out with anxiety. You said you were going to have me arrested, and nothing's happened."

"Well, I may as well tell you the truth; I meant to do so. But other people interfered."

"Who interfered?"

"H'm! You know what women are. There's that daughter of mine, Elise. And she said no."

"That—that's very strange," said Rolandsen.

Mack looked at the telegrams once more. "This is excellent," he said. "Couldn't you give me some idea of the thing itself?"

Rolandsen explained a little of the process.

"That means, we're to some extent competitors," said Mack.

"Not to some extent only. From the moment I've sent off my answer, we're competitors in earnest."

"Eh?" Mack started. "What do you mean? Are you going to set up a factory yourself?"

"Yes. There's water-power higher up, beyond your place, and more of it, and easier to work."

"But that's Levion's water."

"I've bought it."

Mack wrinkled up his forehead thoughtfully. "Good! We're competitors, then," he said.

Said Rolandsen, "That means you will lose."

But Mack, the man of power, was growing more and more offended; he was not accustomed to this sort of thing, and not disposed to put up with it.

"You're strangely forgetful, young man; you keep on forgetting that you're in my power," said he.

"Do as you please. If you lock me up now, my turn will come later, that's all."

"What—what will you do then?"

"Ruin you," said Rolandsen.

Frederik came in. He saw at once that the two had been having words, and it annoyed him that his father did not settle this big-nosed ex-telegraph person out of hand.

Then said Rolandsen aloud, "I will make you an offer: we can take up this invention together. Make the necessary alterations in your factory, and I'll take over the management there. That's my offer—and it holds good for twenty-four hours!"

Whereupon Rolandsen strode out, leaving the telegrams with Mack.

XV

A utumn was setting in; the wind rushing through the woods, the sea yellow and cold, and a great awakening of stars in the sky. But Ove Rolandsen had no time now for watching meteor flights, though he'd as great a fancy as ever for such things. There had been gangs of men at work on Mack's factory of late, pulling down here and setting up there, under orders from Rolandsen, who managed it all. He had settled all difficulties now, and was a man of mark.

"I knew he would get on," said Old Mack. "I believed in him all along."

"I did not," said proud Elise. "The way he goes about now. It's as if he'd been the saving of us all."

"Oh, it's not as bad as that," said Mack.

"He says a word of greeting when he passes, but he never stops for a reply. He just walks on."

"Ah! he's busy, that's all."

"He's sneaked into the family, that's what he's done," said Elise, her lips a little pale. "Wherever we are, he's sure to be there too. But if he's any ideas in his head about me, he's very much mistaken."

Elise went back to town.

And everything went on as usual, as if one could do without her well enough. But it was this way now with Rolandsen: from the time he had entered into partnership with Mack, he had promised himself to do good work and not waste time in dreaming of other things. Dreams and fancies for the summer-time—and then best to stop. But some go dreaming all their lives; go fluttering mothwise all their lives, and never can make an end. Now here was Jomfru van Loos in Bergen. Rolandsen had had a letter from her, to say she didn't really never at all make out as he was beneath her, seeing he hadn't demeaned himself with burglary and thieving after all, but only doing it for monkey tricks and fun. And that she took back her words about breaking it off, if so be it wasn't too late and couldn't be altered.

Elise Mack came home again in October. It was said she was properly engaged now, and her betrothed, Henrik Burnus Henriksen, captain of the coasting vessel, was visiting her. There was to be a grand ball in the great hall at Rosengaard, and a troupe of wandering musicians, on their way down from Finmarken, had been hired to play flutes and trumpets on the night. All the village was invited, Rolandsen with the rest, and Olga was to be there, and be received as Frederik Mack's intended. But the Vicarage people were, unfortunately, prevented. A new chaplain had been appointed, and was expected every day, and the present incumbent, good man, was going elsewhere, up to the northward, where another flock needed his care. He was not altogether displeased to be going away now, to plough and sow new ground; he had not always been happy in his work here. He could look back upon a great deal accomplished; he had got Levion's sister to call to mind the one man who owed her marriage. It was the village carpenter, a house-owner, a man of property, and with money stored under his pillow. When the priest joined them together before the altar, it was with a feeling of satisfaction. After all, unceasing toil might here and there bear fruit among the benighted.

All things came right in time—and praise the Lord, thought the priest. His household was in something nearer order now, the new housekeeper had come, and old and reliable she was;

he would take her with him and keep her on at the new place. All would come right in time, no doubt. The priest had been a hard man to deal with, but none seemed to bear him enmity for that. When he stepped on board down at the waterside, there were many had come to see him off. As for Rolandsen, he would not let slip this opportunity of showing courtesy. Mack's boat was there already with three men, waiting for him, but he would not go on board until the Vicarage folk had gone. In spite of all, the priest could not but thank him for so much consideration. And as Lay-helper Levion had carried the new priest's lady ashore when first they came, so now he carried her on board again as well. Matters were looking brighter now for Levion, too, seeing the priest had undertaken to say a word for his reinstatement in his former post.

All would come right, no doubt.

"Now if you weren't going north and I south," said Rolandsen, "we might go together."

"Yes," said the priest. "But let us remember, my dear Rolandsen, that we may go north and we may go south, but we shall all meet again in one place at the last!" Thus spoke the priest in priestly wise, and was unshaken to the last.

Fruen sat in the stern, wearing the same pitiful shoes; they had been patched, but were grown most heartily ugly thereby. Yet she was not downcast for that; far from it; her eyes shone, and she was joyful at the thought of coming to some new place, to see what there might be. Though she could not help feeling a wistful regret for a big grey pebblestone that her husband would not let her put in her trunk, for all it was so pretty to see.

They pushed off from land, and there was a waving of hats and sou'westers and handkerchiefs, and calling "*Farvel!*" from the boat and from the shore.

Then Rolandsen went on board. He had to be at Rosengaard

that evening; a double engagement was to be celebrated, and here again he could not let slip the chance of being polite. Mack's boat had no pennant at the mast, wherefore he had borrowed a magnificent one of huge dimensions on his own account, and had it hoisted before setting out.

He came to Rosengaard that evening. The great trading station was evidently decked for a festival; there were lights in the windows on both floors, and the ships in the harbour were fluttering their flags, though it was already dark. Rolandsen said to his men, "Go ashore now, and send three others to relieve; I shall be starting back to the factory at midnight."

Frederik Mack came out at once to receive him, and Frederik was in high spirits. He had now every hope of getting that berth as mate; then he would be able to marry, and be something on his own account. Old Mack too was pleased, and wore the decoration given him by the King on the royal visit to Finmarken. Neither Elise nor Captain Henriksen were to be seen—cooing somewhere by themselves, no doubt.

Rolandsen took a glass or so, and set himself to be quiet and strong. He sat down with Old Mack, and talked over various matters of business: this dye-stuff, now, that he had discovered; it had seemed a trifle at first, but already it looked like becoming a main product, perhaps the chief of all. He needed machinery and plant, apparatus for distilling. Elise came by; she looked Rolandsen full in the face and said, "*Godaften*" out loud, and nodded. Rolandsen stood up and bowed, but she walked by.

"She's very busy this evening," said Mack.

"And we shall have to have everything in readiness before the Lofoten fishing begins," said Rolandsen, sitting down again. Ho-ho! He was not to be crushed, not to be in the least put out by any sort of feeling!—"I still think the best thing to do would be to charter a small steamer and send up, with Frederik as master."

"Frederik may be getting another post now. But we can talk it all over to-morrow; there's plenty of time."

"I am going back to-night."

"Nonsense!" said Mack. "There's no earthly need for that."

Rolandsen stood up and said shortly, "At midnight." Firm and inflexible, that was the way.

"Well, really, I had thought you would stay the night. On a special occasion like this. I think I may call it something of a special occasion."

They walked about among the others, stopping to exchange a few words here and there. Rolandsen encountered Captain Henriksen, and they drank together as if they had been old friends, though neither had seen the other before. The Captain was a cheery fellow, a trifle stout.

Then the music struck up, tables were laid in three rooms, and Rolandsen behaved admirably in choosing himself a place well apart from the most distinguished guests. Mack, making a round of the tables, found him there, and said, "What, are you sitting here? Well, now, I was going to...."

Said Rolandsen, "Not at all, thanks very much; we can hear your speech quite nicely from here."

Mack shook his head. "No, I'm not going to make any speech." And he moved off with a thoughtful air, as if something had upset him.

The meal went on; there was much wine, and a great buzz of voices. When the coffee came round, Rolandsen started writing out a wire. It was to Jomfru van Loos in Bergen, to say it was by no means too late and couldn't be altered, come north soonest possible.—Yours, Ove.

And that was well, all things were excellently well— delightful! He went down himself to the station and sent off the wire. Then he went back to the house. There was more life and movement about the tables now; guests changed places; Elise came through to where he sat, and offered her hand. She begged him to excuse her having passed by so hurriedly before.

"If you only knew how lovely you are again this evening," said he, and was calm and polite.

"Do you think so, now?"

"I always did think so. I'm an old admirer of yours, you know. Don't you remember last year, when I actually proposed to you?"

But she did not seem to like his tone now, and went away for the time being. But a little later he came upon her again. Frederik had led out his lady, the dancing had begun, and no one took any notice of a couple talking together.

Said Elise, "Oh, by the way, I've heard from an old acquaintance of yours, Jomfru van Loos."

"Have you, though?"

"She heard I was going to be married, and wants to come and keep house for me. I believe she's a very good housekeeper. But of course you know her better than I do."

"She is very clever, yes. But she can't come and keep house for you."

"Oh...?"

"Seeing I've wired her this evening offering her another post. She's engaged to me now."

Proud Elise started at that, and looked hard at him. "I thought it was over between you," she said.

"Oh, well, you know what they say about old love.... It *was* all over at one time, but now...."

"I see," said Elise.

Then said Rolandsen, magnificently polite, "I can't help saying you've never been so lovely as you are to-night! And then your dress, that dark-red velvet dress...."

He felt very pleased with himself after that speech; no one could ever imagine the least unrest behind it.

"You didn't seem to care so very much for her," said Elise.

He saw that her eyes were dewed, and he winced. A little strangeness in her voice, too, confused him, and the look on his face changed suddenly.

"Where's your splendid coolness now?" she asked, and smiled.

"You've taken it," he said in a low voice.

Then suddenly she stroked his hand, a single touch, and left him. She hurried in through the rooms, seeing none and hearing nothing, only hurrying on. In the passage stood her brother, and he called to her; she turned her all-smiling face full towards him, and the tears dripped from her lashes; then she ran upstairs to her room.

A quarter of an hour later her father came up. She flung her arms round his neck and said, "I can't!"

"Eh? No, no. But you must come down again and dance; they're asking after you. And what have you been saying to Rolandsen? He's changed so all in a moment. Have you been rude to him again?"

"Oh no, no, I wasn't rude to him...."

"Because if you were, you'll have to put it right at once. He's leaving at twelve o'clock to-night."

"Leaving at twelve!" Elise was ready in a moment, and said, "I'm coming down at once."

She went downstairs, and found Captain Henriksen.

"I can't," said she.

He made no answer.

"I dare say it's so much the worse for me, but I simply can't."

"Very well, then," was all he said.

She could not give any further explanation, and the Captain apparently having no more to say, nothing more was said. Elise went down to the telegraph station and telegraphed Jomfru van Loos, Bergen, not to accept Ove Rolandsen's offer, same being again not seriously meant. Await letter.—Elise Mack.

Then she went home and joined the dancers again.

"Is it true you're leaving at twelve to-night?" she asked Rolandsen.

"Yes."

"Then I'm going with you to the factory. I've something to do there."

And she stroked his hand once more.

Notes

13   *Marie van Loos*: Her name is of Dutch origin and she is also described
later on as coming from Bergen, whose citizens are famous for their
distinctive dialect and their cool, haughty demeanour. Her position
becomes her title in the opening paragraph: Hamsun has already called
her *Husjomfru*, the first word of the novel in the original, meaning
housekeeper, but a few sentences later Worster keeps the original,
Jomfru, which has an entirely other meaning of virgin, or maiden,
making that her title in English…!
Rosengaard: Readers of Hamsun's work will be familiar with this place
as the trading place where the various members of the extended Mack
clan are based. Hamsun describes it as being '*en mil borte*', one mile
away, where one Norwegian mile equals ten kilometres, so Worster's
translation is slightly inaccurate, being closer to six English miles.
Interestingly, the setting of this novel is never named.
Nordland: That long narrow stretch of Northern Norway that features
in much of Hamsun's writing and where he moved to as a very young
boy.
The crows…: Worster omits Hamsun's detail: *Skjor og kråke er kommet
langt pa vei…*, The magpies and the crows are getting on fast…
sallows: willows, and in the original is singular, the willow.

14   *skilling*: Hamsun is using the word colloquially to mean something
equivalent to the English 'penny' but these coins were obsolete after
1875 when Norway introduced the *krone* after joining the Scandinavian
Monetary Union.
striding down the road: not Hamsun's words exactly: *Nu kom endelig
store Rolandsen sagte nedover veien…*, Now Big Rolandsen eventually
comes slowly down the road… which seems to create the opposite
impression to Worster's translation.
Bergen: The largest town on the Norwegian west coast and a major
commercial and fishing centre with a unique dialect heavily influenced
by Danish. Jomfru van Loos would have appeared rather exotic to the
natives of the novel.
Jomfru Fan Løs: Worster's own note needs some explanation.

Rolandsen is punning on van/Fa(e)n, which latter element belongs amongst Norwegian's long list of devil-related swear words and Loos/ Løs the place name of a town in Northern France famous from a battle in the First World War and loose. It is difficult to convey this phrase without using much stronger words in English!

15 *The lay-helpers down at the waterside were by no means glad of his company at the moment - at this particular, highly important moment*: Hamsun is much stronger in the original than Worster communicates: *Medhjaelperne nede ved naustene hadde helst set at han ikke var kommet i denne stund...* The lay-helpers down at the boathouses had much rather seen that he had not come at all at this particular moment...
red nose: Hamsun doesn't say he has a red nose at all, but a big one, *Hans store naese...*
Houseboat: not exactly the sort of boat we imagine by the term houseboat, but something stylish that was more than what the fisher folk would use, probably including some accommodation to protect guests in bad weather.
Here they come!: In the original there follows a paragraph that Worster has not included here. Hamsun describes how the servant girls are all in a tizzy over the arrival of the new chaplain and his wife but Jomfru van Loos was here in the last priest's tenure and she doesn't let these sort of things fluster her.
Goddag: Formal, Hello.

16 *Lay-helper Levion wades out*: Levion wades out because this really is a poor place without any landing facilities or pier.
Now if I only knew enough: Hamsun uses the word *kundskapen* and the words might be better translated, *Now, if I just knew who they all were...*
If there won't be any children?: Worster's text suggests something that Hamsun's doesn't, that is, a repetition of the original question, *If there aren't any children?*

17 *the quay*: there is no quay, of course, Hamsun simply says *sjøen*, the sea.

18 *Enok would be sure to bring it about*: it may be that Worster's translation reflects a sense that is not the same to us, namely that Rolandsen's words would be spread around by just this man.
fish-glue: still produced in Norway by boiling down fish carcasses. As well as being a glue it is used in priming, binding and fixing and for the restoration of artworks. Its origins go back well into ancient history.

Old Mick: This is curious. Hamsun writes, *gammel Laban*, which is a biblical reference to Jacob's father-in-law and brother of Rebecca. This has nothing to do with the devil but is rather invective of sorts to describe someone who is a layabout, a liar or a cheat. The girls laugh at him because he is drunk and they think he is confusing Laban with Adam in the original. Hamsun of course is suggesting Adam's role in mythic temptations.

19 *Lensmand*: At the time this novel is set the office is usually held by an important local man taken from the upper levels of the landed farmers' classes and had a number of political, legal, financial and social responsibilities. In modern Norway he is attached to the Police Force.

20 *drink*: Hamsun is a little more careful with his choice of words, *braendevin*, meaning distilled alcohol, often home-made.

21 *Save for his weight of poverty and helplessness, Rolandsen of the Telegraphs....famous by this time*: Here and later on this page Worster shifts the emphasis of Hamsun's words. When Hamsun writes, *Hvis bare ikke telegrafist Rolandsen hadde sin store armod og hjaelpeløshet å stride med skulde opfindelsen nu ha vaeret en kjendsgjaerning*, If Rolandsen the telegraphist simply hadn't had to struggle with his great poverty and helplessness his discovery would by now have become a famous endeavour. Worster makes Rolandsen seem subtly less heroic. And later his phrasing seems odd: *not without motive and vainly*, whereas Hamsun is much more colloquial, *ikke for nul og ingenting*, not for nought or nothing.

22 *coasting steamer*: *kystbåten*, coastal steamer would seem more appropriate.

23 *seiners*: men who manage the seines, a type of dragnet used for catching surface fish that gather in large numbers, probably Hamsun had seen the purse seine being used which can be gathered at the bottom so no fish can escape from below.
    their voyage to Bergen with dried fish: Hamsun is much more accurate: *efter klipfiskturen til Lofoten*, after the cod fishing trip out to the Lofoten islands. What he means is the annual fishing trips out for cod that were then dried and salted to produce *klippfisk*, saltcod, and sailed south to Bergen and from there exported around the world.

24 *daler*: *speciedaler*, colloquially as *daler*, were the currency of Norway from 1816 to 1875.

25 *Something had to be done*: Worster's own insertion.
    Nicodemus: He was a Pharisee who is famous for a night-time

conversation with Jesus that prompts important discussions about being born again and the nature of the afterlife. This tenuous link the new priest's uses in his sermon to rail against the thief in the night.

26 *and stood there on board with his red sash round his waist*: for some reason Worster neglects to include Hamsun's added detail, *i pels*, in a fur coat. Mack is wearing a fur coat even though it is midsummer.

27 *the spokesman of the village*: Hamsun calls him an *ordfører*, mayor.

28 *Proud and haughty she was, and carried herself like a lady*: Worster seems to have transferred this to Elise here, because Hamsun wrote this part of the sentence about Rolandsen: *Han var stolt og stornaeset og kunde opfore sig*; He was proud and big-nosed and knew how to behave properly. The contrast between original text and translator's text is remarkable.

I saw the telegraph people at Rosengaard before I left: what Hamsun wrote explains Rolandsen's reaction much more: *Jeg kan hilse frå telegrafisterne på Rosengaard*, I can say 'Hello' from the telegraph people at Rosengard.

31 *maid*: Hamsun means maiden, young woman.

33 *What! cried Jomfru van Loos…*: This little exchange has a different edge in Hamsun's original. Marie's question is more of an outburst and not a question, she doesn't repeat the word *What?* and Rolandsen's response is much more of an active statement, *Se pa meg, viser jeg noget slags tegn til uro om våren?* Look at me, do I show any sign of restlessness in the spring?

Bergen dialect: Worster's translation conveys the humour of Hamsun's little joke but the effect in Norwegian is slightly different and based on the use of *en*, one, with *enestående*, unique, so she describes the priest as 'one of the unique preachers I have ever heard'. Of course, what is much funnier is the fact that Rolandsen takes no notice of what she is saying about his preaching.

35 *Four hundred Speciedaler*: it is difficult to be absolutely accurate but a month's wage for many was probably around 2 dalers a month at that time and so four hundred is a fortune. Nowadays this sum may be worth something like £8,500.

37 *She could always find some use for….and such things*: Worster misses out from the list *tandpulver*, toothpowder (toothpaste) and *piper til å blåse i*, pipes to puff on.

40 *Two or three thousand! said Fruen. Only fancy!*: What she really says is slightly different, rather less excitable: *Taenk, to, tre tusen! sier fruen,*

Imagine, two, three thousand! said the lady. Here and in other places Worster adds the phrasing of a naïve, middle-class English lady which she isn't, she is slightly more laconic than that.

43 *Lensmandsgaard*: *gaard* is a farm or a small group of farmhouses.
It was weather for dreams; for little fluttering quests of the heart: Hidden in here is a clue to the title of the novel: *Det var veir til å flagre i, å svaerme i.* This was weather to flutter in, to swarm in. Hamsun is suggesting floating, idling, doing nothing in particular with the first verb and punning on dreams and what butterflies do with the second. Worster adds something more overtly romantic in his version.
Ove Rolandsen too felt the spell: Hamsun echoes the words above here that Worster doesn't convey: *Også Ove Rolandsen svaermet på sin måte.* In his own way Ove Rolandsen also swarmed/dreamed.

44 *Ort*: One speciedale was exchanged for 4 kroner in 1877 under the new monetary system and one *ort* was exchanged for 80 øre (100 øre in one krone). Hamsun seems to deliberately have placed the time frame back a generation or two before the book was published in 1904.

50 *Fröken*: Miss, but with slightly more sense of conferring status, certainly in the generations before Hamsun set his novel the term would have been used much more for aristocratic ladies.

51 *His breast was a whirl of strange feelings*: Hamsun explains why with a sentence that Worster chooses to leave out. V*armen av den fløiels hånd hadde faret i ham*, The warmth of that velvet hand coursed through him.

53 *the knob of a head he bore on his shoulders*: rather unfortunate connotations in modern colloquial English but Worster is conveying the semantics of Hamsun's word, *knap*, turned wood, end of a stick, a button.
from Lofoten to Finmarken: from the western edge of Northern Norway to the eastern. Worster leaves the definite article on the place name, Finmarken, the Finmark.

55 *these interchanges creditable*: not quite the appropriate register for either the situation or Hamsun's earthy original: *det var talt godt på begge sider*, literally, it was well said on both sides, better, they were both bragging as good as each other.
the other's coat: Worster keeps the pace but misses out on a little detail: Hamsun uses the word, *gasten* here, rather than simply *the other*, to describe Ulrik and the other seamen, a Danish word meaning a seaman of low rank who turns up for the single journey.

58 *his wife in the adjoining room*: the fact that they have separate rooms points to considerably higher status than their fellows in the village who would probably be living in one- or two-roomed houses where everything was shared.

61 *tollekniv*: sheath knife, *tolle* from *telgja*, to whittle.

Offering: originally, *offerdag*, sacrifice days, when sacrificed animals would be given to the church as a form of tax but by this time an opportunity to contribute to the collection for the benefit of the priest.

70 *the instrument*: Worster means the telegraph.

78 *That was the end of Ove Rolandsen*: not quite the same hopelessness in Hamsun's own words: *Der var Ove Rolandsen havnet*, And that was where Ove Rolandsen had ended up.

It was not the place a man of any decent position could choose to live in: Hamsun's sentence carries much more the pithy weight of a Viking saying: *Ingen bedre man burde bo der*, No better man ought to live there.

Midsummer's eve came round, and fires were lit on high places: In Norwegian, *Sankt Hans* or *Jonsok*. This is clearly a Christianised pagan festival of midsummer, celebrated throughout northern Europe with large bonfires, wild dancing, drinking and singing the old songs. Despite the Church's best efforts it remains an important event in the Norwegian calendar.

drunk as an owl: strangely enough Hamsun compares him to another bird, *fuld som en alke*, drunk as a razorbill, a not uncommon idiom, probably because of their peculiarly listing walk.

80 *It was beautiful to see him…*: The emphasis is different in the Norwegian: *Det var et ganske skjønt traek hos Levion…* It was a rather attractive characteristic of Levion's that he…

81 *These midsummer bonfires are dangerous*: Hamsun lets the priest use the moment to get in a dig against these heathen practices: *Disse Sankt Hans bål er en fordaervelig skik*, These St. John's bonfires are a depraved custom. Worster bowdlerises when he feels sensitive issues arising.

89 *dog-days*: hundedagene, the dog days: not fixed, but a period of perhaps 40 days of hot, sultry weather from the middle of July to the end of August so named because in the ancient world they were associated with the rising of Sirius in the constellation of Canis Major.

the Russians were at war: if Hamsun is referring to a real war in the fifty years leading up to the publication of the novel he may mean the Crimean War, 1853–56, otherwise Russia was only involved in that period in minor wars.

90 *for the abolishment of Rolandsen*: Hamsun focuses more on the verbal battle that the priest is preparing for, *målbinde* is the word he uses, to render someone speechless, to shut someone up.

94 *Shouldn't think anyone'd care to keep food in a thing like that*: Rolandsen doesn't mention the food that might be in the box in Hamsun's original, he is a little more circumspect: *Den burde ikke gå an å ha noget i den*: It shouldn't really be possible to have anything in it.

95 *Hamburg*: as a major centre of the Hanseatic League, Hamburg would have connections with Bergen and the Atlantic coast of Norway.

96 *Better come again later on, said Frederik... Frederik shrugged his shoulders*: this small section here is compressed by Worster into three lines from Hamsun's seven. First of all Rolandsen gives up and then says, Yes, yes and sets off walking, then he starts to bite his lips together and turns back and then says, When I came here it was simply to meet no one else other than your father, do you understand?

100 *Rolandsen's big nose looked even more aggressive*: Worster adds aggressive in his translation, Hamsun simply says his nose looks even bigger than normal, *Han så endda mere stornaeset ut nu end før i tiden*, He looked even more big-nosed now than earlier.
Fish-glue: Hamsun writes *fischleim*, German because of the nature of the correspondence Mack is reading.

103 *Dreams and fancies for the summer-time—and then best to stop. But some go dreaming all their lives; go fluttering mothwise all their lives...*: *Man svaermer om sommeren, så holder man op for den gang. Men nogen svaermer hele sit liv...* One dreams in summer, then one stops. But some dream all their lives... Worster's translation here is full of poetic licence.

104 *Rolandsen had had a letter from her..*: what follows from here on in this paragraph is Worster creating the language of a typical English, lower-class Housekeeper affecting 'proper' grammar with its double negatives and hyper-correct grammar which is not present in Hamsun's Norwegian.

106 *Godaften*: Good evening, but polite and Danish-ified, rather than the more rustic and Norwegian, *God kveld*.

About the Author

~

KNUT HAMSUN was born in Gudbrandsdalen, Norway, in 1859 and grew up in poverty in Hamarøy in Nordland. In early childhood he was apprenticed to a shoemaker, later working as a road builder, stonemason, and a school teacher. He spent several years in America, travelling and working as a tram driver, and these experiences were published under the title *Fra det moderne Amerikas Aandsliv* (1889) (*The Intellectual Life of Modern America*). His novels *Sult* (1890) (*Hunger*) and *Pan* (1894) led to his literary breakthrough. Hamsun was awarded the Nobel Prize for Literature in 1920 for his masterpiece *Markens Grøde* (1917) (*Growth of the Soil*). He died on February 19, 1952.

RICHARD ECCLES studied Old Norse at university. He has lived and worked in Norway and Iceland, and travelled across many parts of Scandinavia. Hamsun's writing has been a lifelong interest.

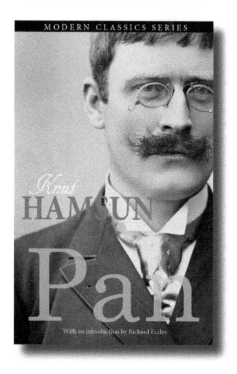

MODERN CLASSICS SERIES

Knut
HAMSUN
Pan

With an introduction by Richard Eccles

First published in Norwegian in 1894, *Pan* tells the story of Lieutenant Thomas Glahn's life and adventures in a remote township in northern Norway, a scene described by Richard Eccles in his poignant introduction as 'that remote, exotic, romantic, difficult landscape of extreme and epic beauty at the top of the world...'

This stunning new edition restores translator W. Worster's powerful recreation of Hamsun's enigmatic original and includes an informative introduction and notes by Richard Eccles.

'The whole modern school of fiction in the twentieth century stems from Hamsun.'
Isaac Bashevis Singer

Ingram Content Group UK Ltd.
Milton Keynes UK
UKHW011858240423
420698UK00008B/561